Books by A.J. Llewellyn

Pearl Harbor

I0546053

Vagabond Heart
Gypsy Heart
Abiding Heart
Avenging Heart

Elemental Superpowers

The Cake
The Blancmange
The Mudpie

Tiki Vampires

Fever
Fever Pitch
Fever Quenched

Blood Slave: Nibiru Vampire Warriors

Nibiru Vampire Warriors: Chapter One
Nibiru Vampire Warriors: Chapter Two
Nibiru Vampire Warriors: Chapter Three
Nibiru Vampire Warriors: Chapter Four
Nibiru Vampire Warriors: Chapter Five
Nibiru Vampire Warriors: Chapter Six
Nibiru Vampire Warriors: Chapter Seven
Nibiru Vampire Warriors: Chapter Eight
Nibiru Vampire Warriors: Chapter Nine
Nibiru Vampire Warriors: Chapter Ten
Nibiru Vampire Warriors: Chapter Eleven

Nibiru Vampire Warriors: Chapter Twelve

Cloaks and Daggers

Stavros

Haunted By You

Tall With Room

Oberon's Court

Sex and Candy

Titania's Court

Orange Crush

Sexy Snax

The Mediator
Shipwreck Bay

Anthologies

Emergency Servicing
Sins of Summer

Single Titles

Stealing Rain
Paper Valentine
Burnt Island
Full
If Come
Roley's Wood
The Kaupe
Hanalei Moon

Wolf Moon
Beyond the Reef
The Bouncer
The Pirate Fairy

The Pirate Fairy

ISBN # 978-1-78651-358-8

©Copyright A.J. Llewellyn 2016

Cover Art by Posh Gosh ©Copyright 2016

Interior text design by Claire Siemaszkiewicz

Pride Publishing

Published in 2016 by Pride Publishing, Newland House, The Point, Weaver Road, Lincoln, LN6 3QN, United Kingdom.

THE PIRATE FAIRY

A.J. LLEWELLYN

Dedication

Dedicated to my wonderful friend Gary Hill, in honor of the lengthy discussions and passions we share about adventuring in the high seas. Aloha Nui xxxx

Chapter One

1841

Somewhere on the high seas...

"Don't hurt me," the naked young man whimpered.

Denny kissed his captive's smooth cheek, inhaling his masculine fragrance. Denny detected a hint of soap beneath some kind of woodsy oil on his skin. The young man's fear spiced up the sheen on his muscles. He groaned as Denny squeezed his biceps.

"I'm not gay," the young man insisted.

Denny chuckled. "That's what they all say."

The young man bit his lip, but writhed toward Denny's probing fingers, not away from them, igniting Denny's passions anew. He ran his hand down the young man's face. A knocking sound came from somewhere, distracting him.

Ignore it. They'll go away. He slid his hand across the young man's throat, letting his fingers pause to feel the quickened pulse. Denny kept moving down the smooth, taut torso. He couldn't resist handling the juicy, buoyant cock begging for his touch. He cuffed the young man's shaft with his fingers, trying to hold the blue-eyed gaze before him, but the knocking continued.

What's the use? It's just a dream anyway. I'll never get him back.

Prince Merritt.

Only in his dreams did Denny allow himself to utter his name. He still couldn't believe he'd lost his beloved prisoner. He rarely dreamed about Merritt anymore.

Even if I saw him again, he wouldn't want me the way I look now.

The knocking intensified.

Burrowing his head deeper under the covers, Denny fought to return to his twilight world, enjoying the temptations awaiting him there. And there they were. How wonderful. It hardly ever happened that he returned to the exact moment he'd been interrupted in a dream, but Merritt's smile drew him in once more. His blond-haired lover smiled, beckoning him. The bashing on his cabin door grew so loud the bed shook, wrestling Denny Derrick Dalton with a jolt from his sleep. So annoying, too, right in the middle of the good part about his captive prince chained up in stowage, and Denny about to shove his cock up Merritt's ass.

This had become his favorite dream, but one often denied him. One so real he could feel the excited prince's breath on his face, his feverish, whispered words, 'Please don't hurt me,' the very things that made Denny want to do wicked, wanton things to the tethered male beauty.

But the insistent rapping continued, and Denny had to come back to reality. And for the furious pirate captain of the La-Di-Da, reality wasn't so hot these days.

"Cap'n. Sir. There's a boat up ahead," came the timid voice from the other side of the door.

Denny stirred in his bed. Once again he'd made a mess of the bedding, and for a moment he hated what had happened to him so much that he wanted to find that—

"Sir? Are you in there? There's a boat." The voice rose to a squeaky pitch.

"I heard ya. Keep your breeches on."

"But they *are* on, sir."

He knew now it was Sorenson, the stranded Swedish idiot he'd picked up in Port Victoria, in the Seychelles. Sorenson, the alleged cook who'd bought rancid flour from a tradesman with a fake mustache and an indecipherable

8

accent. Sorenson had thought the bits of black stuff in it was caraway seeds and not weevils and rat droppings.

"So? What's the big deal? Attack it. Do I have to do everything around here?" Irritated, Denny punched his pillow, rolled over on his stomach and stared balefully out of the porthole. He'd expected it to be early morning but was surprised to see the sun high and probably hot. He hadn't left his quarters much in the last three months, and his sheets were getting a bit stinky.

It suddenly occurred to him. *Why's the cook coming up here? Why isn't he making my porridge? Where is everybody else?*

A second voice piped up, "But, sir. Cap'n. Sir. There are thirteen of 'em, sir. Fishing boats. All like sittin' ducks in the port, like."

Denny rolled his eyes. Parlayne Foster was his first mate and originally from New England, where they'd been headed for two weeks after bad storms steered them from Honduras, their original planned destination. Foster, however, had taken to his new life so well he and Sorenson had started talking like all the other Cockney gits Denny employed. And this from a Bostonian missionary's son.

Thirteen vessels? Denny's cock got hard. Only two things aroused him these days. A hot young man's ass wanting a royal fucking, and multiple vessels awaiting his attack. Fishing boats meant fish, and probably gold.

"Hoist the flag," he yelled and got up out of bed. He visited the head then contemplated his wardrobe. He had to look the part. Tight black pants, thigh-high boots, crisp white shirt with a few ruffles. Aye. That was the ticket. It was easy getting on pants, but negotiating socks was difficult. He had no balance. He got so frustrated he stuffed his boots on, and with the scrunched-up socks inside, he fell down. Unbelievable. He'd been so sure the curse would have worn off by now, but it hadn't. He slipped on the shirt and wanted to cry. He'd had to put two slits in the back to accommodate his new deformity. It just wasn't fair. On top of this he threw on a long coat. That kept his little problem well hidden.

Outside the cabin, he inhaled fresh ocean air for the first time in weeks and almost keeled over in shock. He caught the gazes of a couple of deck hands. Both seemed surly. He'd spent years on the high seas with both of them, fucking them alternately and occasionally together. Denny had rejected both since the dreadful curse had hit him. He'd shunned all human contact. The only good thing about their grumpy expressions was that it seemed that Foster hadn't told the entire crew of his misfortune.

Denny took a deep breath and climbed the companionway up to the deck. He'd forgotten how gorgeous the ocean was first thing in the morning. It glistened like glass and he could have allowed himself to become mesmerized, but he had work to do. He surveyed the deck of the La-Di-Da, a former British Navy privateer. Spotless. It had once been named for Queen Victoria, but Denny, a former midshipman who had staged a mutiny two years ago, before the ship had reached India, had renamed it. He'd always had a notion he should have been born in high places, and not in the shameful East London dump where he'd rubbed with others grouped as The Great Wen.

He tried to picture himself walking down the streets of his old neighborhood with his new affliction and couldn't. For one thing he was unable to control his, er, condition. For another, he'd always prided himself on his good looks. Dark-haired, dashing, handsome.

Cursed.

Damn.

Denny felt the weight of the crew's watchful gazes on his back. Maybe they did know. His whammy made him looked hunchbacked. And who'd ever heard of a hunchbacked pirate?

He nodded at the few crewmen scattered around him. Denny had never liked taking orders, but he *adored* giving them. Denny had plotted against his ship's captain, Lester Piggins, from day one. Denny had left England eight years ago at the ripe old age of seventeen, under dubious circumstances. His good looks, impressive stature and fearless protection of the crew had ensured that all one hundred and fifty of them had chosen to stay with him when he'd accomplished his mission two years later. One hundred and fifty one, if you counted Theodore, the formerly starving kitten that had stowed away on the ship during a brief call into the port of Diego-Suarez in Madagascar.

Renaming the ship the La-Di-Da, Denny thought, was a good laugh at his former delusions of grandeur. He was no upper-class twit. In his heart of hearts he wished he were. And in some ways, he adopted their mannerisms. Not to mention their clothes and money. He robbed the rich and gave constantly to the poor, as in himself and his crew. They had set off to seek their fortune and to terrorize other ships in the Indian Ocean. They had done both with a beautiful success rate for five years now, thanks to the two tanks and sixty guns on board plus those they stole in their frequent attacks. They'd also been helped by the increased speed of the La-Di-Da, following a complete restructuring of the vessel on the small island of Ruatan off the coast of Honduras.

A year ago, Denny Derrick Dalton had come up with the brilliant idea, which increasingly seemed less so, to switch his activities to the North Atlantic Ocean. He'd managed to hide gold in various caves throughout the Caribbean and had even bought a house on a hill above the seaside in Cornwall, England. He'd looked forward to an early retirement, until he'd been cursed. Things had gone from bad to worse since rescuing Prince Merritt and his sister. Sisters were bad news. Denny knew that from experience. But Merritt's sister was the worst.

Damn that woman. I can't retire until I find her and make her take her whammy off me. Aware now of all the crew members' scrutiny, Denny frowned at Sorenson. "Where's my porridge?" he fumed.

11

"But, sir." Sorenson pointed a shaky finger at the boats in the far distance.

"We have time," Denny snapped. He did not add, *Unless you'd prefer to walk the plank,* because the last time he'd threatened, somebody had elected to walk it. The intended victim had somehow managed to survive the initial plunge. Denny had decided not to order the crew to have cannonballs tied to the man's feet. He hadn't been bound or blindfolded either. Denny had done it to teach him a lesson but the man had refused to come back on board. He'd swum away laughing at Denny. It had upset everybody. Nobody knew if the man had survived after the initial drop but several of the crewmembers were upset by the incident. And today, there was no time for hard feelings. There was, however, always time for porridge.

Sorenson scuttled away. Satisfied, Denny studied the map his second mate, Rigby, spread out before him.

Foster handed him a telescope and Denny put it to his eye and peered across the bay. He couldn't see a darned thing. Everything was fuzzy and weird. He scrunched his eye hard but it only made things worse. *I'm falling apart! That curse has done me in! Now I can't bloody see out of my eyes!*

"You're looking through the wrong end," Rigby whispered to him. Rigby was the token Australian aboard and the only man Denny trusted. Rigby was a solid type who told it as he saw it. He liked his ale a little too well, but who didn't?

"Ah," Denny said and flipped the telescope around. He was certain he heard a few crewmembers snickering. Before his affliction, they'd never had reason to mock him. He'd made certain to hide himself as much as possible since disaster had befallen him. Only two of them had seen his… shame.

He took a deep breath and looked again. And there they were. Thirteen boats sheltering at anchor in Port Rosewater. He lowered the telescope, checked the map, looked up at the boats again then back at the map. *Port Rosewater?* Where the hell was that? He tried to decipher the numerous hand jottings on the map. He didn't recognize anything. Not a single name. Even the longitude and latitude coordinates resembled no place he'd ever sailed, and Denny had covered a lot of ocean water in his time.

He gulped. Could he ask Rigby where they were? *Nah. He'll think I've really lost the plot.* Denny sensed tension around him. *I'm being paranoid. Of course they're tense. We're about to take on thirteen boats.*

"Where the hell's my porridge?" he roared.

Sorenson scuttled back to him, a battered metal bowl in one hand, and a spoon in the other. Why were the lad's hands shaking?

Denny peered into the milky-looking sludge. "I hope those black things doing the back stroke in my porridge are raisins," Denny said.

Sorenson winced and shrugged. "Sorry, sir. No. A rat infestation."

"It's rat poop?" Danny thought he'd throw up on the spot. "Where the devil is that cat? Why isn't he earning his keep?"

"He disappeared, sir."

"Disappeared?" Denny gaped at him. "What's that supposed to mean?"

They all looked at him then, cutting glances to and fro between them, then back at Denny.

"What?" he asked Rigby. If anyone could be trusted to spit out the truth it would be him. "What is it?"

"Nothing." Rigby's gaze shifted from side to side, and he added, "Sir," as though it were an afterthought.

"Take it away," Denny roared, pushing the bowl of porridge back toward Sorenson.

"Are we ready to prepare for attack, sir?" Rigby seemed annoyed.

"Yes, but I'd love a cup of coffee."

"Later," Rigby snapped.

"Okay." The boats were getting a bit closer but Denny did

13

love his cup of morning coffee. As long as it didn't have rat poo in it.

"Awaiting your instructions, sir." Rigby's facial expression was neutral.

Denny didn't know what to make of it, because he sensed Rigby's seething fury beneath his flat vocal tone. "Where are we?" he whispered to his second mate.

Rigby gave him an odd look and said something that was obscured by a frigate bird's wild cry. There must have been fish on the boats in the distance. They were always attracted to boats carrying fish. Rigby said something like, "Date with destiny." What did that mean? Was it the name of one of the boats? Denny's head throbbed. Was he still sleeping? Nothing made sense. Maybe Rosewater Bay was part of some bigger port with a name like Bay of Destiny. Maybe that's what he'd heard. Some of these ports had very strange names, but he was afraid to ask Rigby in case his second mate thought Denny was losing his hearing, his eyesight, and his damned marbles.

He took a gamble. "Excellent," Denny said, feeling for the familiar knife in his pocket. "All hands!" he yelled. "All hands on deck! Hoist the flag!"

His crew yelled back acknowledgments and ran around doing his bidding.

"Fire the cannons!" he roared. He loved saying that, even though the actual firing made his ears ring for days. They currently had no prisoners. Denny was wary of taking on anymore after the last bloody catastrophe. The black pirate flag rose high as the first cannon boomed.

Denny felt better than he had in ages. Except he was hot. Damned hot. He wished he could shed the coat but knew he couldn't. Nobody could see the horrors that lay beneath it. His beautiful ship surged forward toward the doomed vessels and he smiled widely until he glimpsed one of his crew running past him. As soon as the man became aware of Denny's scrutiny he gave a strange whimpering sound, clapped a hand over his badly swollen right ear and tiptoed backward away from Denny.

"What's he doing? And what happened to his ear?" Denny demanded of Rigby who sighed.

"You don't remember?"

"No. What am I supposed to remember?"

"You tried to have sex with his ear last night."

"I— What?"

"You heard. You broke into his bunk and tried sticking your cock in his ear. I had to thunk you over the head to get you to stop."

Denny frowned at him. "Is that why I feel like utter shit this morning?"

"No. That'd be all the *la féeverte* you've been drinking." A hint of malice Denny had never seen before danced in Rigby's eyes.

Denny's mouth opened and closed. He had nothing intelligent to say but, since a comment seemed to be required, he mumbled a feeble, "Oh." He was certain Rigby had used these words deliberately, *la féeverte*, or the green fairy, which was the folk name given to absinthe. The green-tinged one-hundred-and-forty-eight proof alcohol had been the only thing that could lift Denny's, er, spirits in his dark days of late. The only trouble being that, tasty as it was, it had been accused of being a powerful hallucinogenic.

I might have to stop drinking that stuff. Why would I try to have sex with somebody's ear? I know I'm a horny git, but this is ridiculous! And the guy isn't even handsome! I wish my bloody affliction was a figment of my imagination but it isn't. Why me? Why the bloody hell did it happen to me?

He ignored the answer that came to his mind. He knew why. He just couldn't get over the reason. And, he never would. He decided to play along with his crew, though the word *mutiny* flittered into his mind. *Nah. They would never do that.* Thanks to him, they were richer men than they'd ever dreamed possible. They angled closer to the fishing boats, and Denny stared. They weren't fishing boats.

Holy guacamole. They were blackbirding boats!

15

As in slave traders!

"We can't rescue all them slaves," Denny said to Rigby, reverting to the ill-bred language of his youth. They couldn't do it, even though he wanted to. Denny Derrick Dalton abhorred slavery, but he could see dozens of dark faces and they worried him. He couldn't fit them all on the La-Di-Da, and some of them looked very ill.

Rigby gave him a harsh laugh. "We're not here to save the slaves."

"We're not?" Denny stared at him.

"No. We've come to sell *you* to the traders. Your wings are the talk of the high seas. Good luck, Captain. You great big bloody fairy, you!"

Denny opened his mouth, but Rigby snatched the telescope out of his hand and swung it hard and close, knocking Denny so viciously, his head snapped to the left. Denny grabbed hold of the instrument to stop Rigby from hitting him again. This time, Rigby hauled back and shot Denny with a right hook to his left temple. It was the last thing he remembered. Denny sank into an instant, befuddled nightmare where the beautiful young girl who'd tried to bed him turned into an old crone when he'd confessed he preferred men.

"You're beautiful," he'd said with a moan. "But I just don't fancy you."

She'd gone bonkers. Maybe he shouldn't have told her he was in love with her brother, but Denny had always prided himself on his passion for honesty. She'd run around his cabin screaming and hurling things, some of them aimed at his head and groin. She'd turned old, her hands going first. They'd looked like crooked, veined talons by the time she'd turned a long, gray finger toward him.

"I banish you to a lifetime of shadow and light, where you will learn to use your wings. Or not." She'd unleashed a dirty cackle. "I'm turning the fairy into a fairy." She'd cackled again, then howled with joy.

Denny had tried to think of it as a dream. A very, very bad

16

one. And she'd lied. There'd been no light in his new world. Just shadows and the fearsome things he sometimes saw out of the corner of his eye. Strange specters, the ghosts of men and women. Theodore, the cat, had hissed at him and run out of the cabin.

The witch-woman had turned back into a young beauty, but her hands had taken longer to change into their former youthful smoothness. She'd put on her cloak and hidden them under the folds, leaving him locked in his cabin. She had plunged him into perpetual night. And he couldn't fly. His wings hurt whenever he stretched them. He always felt them, whether awake or asleep. They seemed to sense things before he did, if he allowed them to transmit messages to him.

He didn't have to try hard to interpret the soft, whispery words they sent him now as he came to, carried by his own men from the La-Di-Da across the wooden plank he'd built himself. They dumped him onto the deck of a blackbirder. Denny spotted the side of his beloved ship and saw that her name had once again been changed. Written in green paint were the words, *The Pirate Fairy.*

Denny Derrick Dalton knew he was in trouble. Deep, dark, trouble.

Chapter Two

Merritt didn't feel like much of a prince, more like his sister's prisoner. He had no choice but to be with Fortunata, and some days she was in such a good mood, their sparkly palace seemed the most wonderful place in the world. Other days, he wished he could escape. But he could never go anywhere for long. She always found him, questioned him, and would scream and yell if she suspected Merritt was moping.

"Stop thinking about *him*!" she'd shriek. But it was difficult. He missed Denny terribly. He'd tried sneaking messages out of the palace via his household staff to seamen whose vessels turned up at the secret island where he and Fortunata lived, but most were intercepted by those loyal to her. Merritt kept hoping one of his notes would make its way to the crew of the La-Di-Da and into Denny's hands.

But then what? If Denny read the note and hoped to rescue Merritt, how could he do so? His sister had so many enchantments on the palace and its immediate surroundings that he would never get inside its walls. Or, maybe he could. Denny was a cunning man. Smart, principled and, Merritt was certain, devoted to him.

Day and night Merritt dreamed of Denny, of the too-brief joy they'd shared. He feared for his lover's safety because he knew Fortunata had cursed him, and lately, he'd been experiencing troubled dreams. Early one morning, his manservant, Elvin, awakened him.

"She's gone, master. Not for long, but she's gone!"

"My sister?" Merritt opened his eyes wider. The room was still dark. When Elvin nodded, he asked, "What time is it?"

"Five o'clock in the morning. She's gone to the forest." Elvin bit his lip, afraid, it seemed.

"Thank you." Merritt threw back his bedclothes. He'd been wondering about Fortunata's half-day disappearances on the mornings before a full moon rose each month. He'd paid Elvin with small bags of gold to follow her. For several weeks now, Merritt had known his sister was visiting a witch in the forest, soliciting information on Denny's whereabouts.

Why is she so obsessed with him? And why is Elvin acting so weird?

"She will kill me if she finds out," Elvin whispered. He might have been the chief elf in their district, but Elvin was like a limp noodle where Fortunata was concerned. She was a cruel mistress to fairy folk, but Merritt adored them all.

"Fortunata will never know. I can promise you that." Merritt reached into his bedside table and extracted a small silken purse filled with gold. He pressed it into Elvin's hands. "Take it. You've earned it."

Elvin shook his head. "No, my lord. I have not. I was too afraid to follow her this time."

"I will follow her. Alone."

"Thank you, my lord." Elvin kept staring at the treasure. "Are you sure?" His small green eyes flickered with a mixture of panic and hopefulness as he gazed up at Merritt.

"Of course. You are very loyal to me, Elvin. I never forget that."

Most of the household staff were too afraid of Fortunata to stand up to her, and sometimes she withheld wages out of spite. Merritt always found a way to secretly pay everybody, but Elvin had three sickly sons that no magic seemed to cure. Merritt was determined to find a way to help them.

Across the room, he pulled his old trunk from against the wall. Filled with souvenirs from his ocean travels, it made a convenient hiding place for the peasant's robes and pants he kept hidden inside a loose floorboard beneath it. He dressed quickly as Elvin watched him. Elvin never helped, at Merritt's insistence. That way, Fortunata could never accuse him of aiding and abetting Merritt in what she would deem subterfuge.

Merritt looked over at him. "Please don't worry. All will be well."

Elvin swallowed. "Here. I almost forgot. I brought you bread and cheese and an apple." He produced a paper parcel from his pocket.

"I feel a bit like Snow White." Merritt grinned at him. "Off to visit the wicked witch."

Elvin sniffed. "And it's not too far from the truth. And at least we know this apple isn't poisoned."

Neither man said anything. It was well known that Fortunata frequently cast horrible spells on people and food, just to maintain control. Merritt's love for his people was the only reason he stayed here. Otherwise he'd have built a raft and gone to look for his lost pirate.

Denny.

Just thinking about him pained Merritt's heart. He took the package of food and squeezed Elvin's shoulder. "Fear not. I shall return." And with that, he took off. Outside, when he was certain nobody was looking, he went into the barn. Avery, his favorite stable hand, was brushing down the magnificent quarter horse, Cillian.

"Who's been riding?" Merritt asked, surprised.

"The princess." Avery had the same glum expression everybody had when they mentioned her.

"She's returned?" Merritt panicked.

"No, sir. She forgot to tie up Cillian and he came running back here."

Even the horses hate her.

"He was shaky and covered in sweat."

Merritt sighed. "She rode him hard. As usual. Don't worry. I'll take him back to her."

"But—"

"She'll never know. I can't have her blaming you when she was clearly distracted."

Avery hesitated. "Are you sure?"

People always said this when Fortunata was the subject of discussion.

"Yes, I'm sure. I'll walk him back to wherever she went."

"You can ride him, sir. Cillian loves you."

"And I love him." It was true. Merritt was an animal lover and took the care and comfort of all the creatures in his kingdom to heart. Cillian gave a gentle whinny, turned and put his muzzle into the palm of Merritt's hand.

Avery smiled as Merritt sighed. Cillian was the most adorable creature. The sensation of the beautiful horse's soft mouth on his skin always centered and calmed him.

"I'll be gentle with him," Merritt promised.

"You always are, sir, and he can handle your sister. I suspect he came home because he loathes being away from you."

"Thank you." Merritt saddled the horse and before he could even ask Cillian to take him to the forest, he took off, Merritt hanging on for dear life.

Cillian was a spirited, joyful creature. His sheer pleasure at running through the trees, along the edge of a rippling brook, then past a field of wild ponies had Merritt laughing as he gripped the reins.

At last they arrived in the only dark spot in the woods.

The witch's house.

Cillian's ears twitched as he bent his knees, allowing Merritt to climb from his back. Merritt took a deep breath, then, as his feet touched the ground, he patted the horse's luxurious mane.

"Thank you, Cillian," he whispered.

Cillian looked at him, his brown eyes alive with warmth and understanding. Merritt studied the house a moment. He could hear a pair of female voices and it didn't sound like a happy conversation. *Oh dear.* Fortunata was frustrated.

"But can you see him?" she yelled.

"Oh yes. I can see him." The second voice sounded weary.

"Well, what's going on?" Fortunata demanded.

"Just one moment." A pause.

"Well?"

Merritt reached into his pocket and removed the package of food Elvin had given him. He removed the apple, thrilled when Cillian threw his head up and down. Cillian adored fruit. Merritt rewrapped the package and fumbled for his pocket knife. He quartered the apple and fed each section to Cillian, who expertly ate the flesh and spat out the seeds. Merritt had never seen another horse do that.

Putting his finger to his lips, as though to shush Cillian, Merritt crept toward the house. He hovered below the witch's window and was stunned when he raised himself a little and saw her scrying inside a large bowl of inky blue water. Merritt held his breath when a shimmering image emerged of Denny lying on the deck of a ship. He had wings. *Oh no.* Fortunata had bewitched him. They'd left the ship so fast that Merritt had been unable to speak to him. Fortunata had spiked a tonic she'd given Merritt and it had left him sleepy for days.

Fortunata poked at the corner of the wavering picture of Denny. She evidently spotted the black cross in the corner at the same moment Merritt did.

"What's that X for?" Fortunata asked.

Gremma drew a sharp breath. Merritt studied her for the first moment. She was young. He knew that because he was aware of her real identity. He gulped. So this was what their long-lost cousin, Gremma, looked like. *Did Fortunata bewitch her? This looks like her handiwork. She's fond of giving people warts. Especially attractive women.*

It shocked him how hideous Gremma had become, her hair gray with white and red streaks through it. She had gnarled hands and huge, snaggled teeth. Dark bushy brows met above the bridge of her bulbous nose, which was covered in warts.

"The X means he's marked for death," Gremma

murmured.

"Good!" Fortunata clapped her hands together.

"If you say so, my lady." Gremma looked dubious.

Fortunata opened her mouth but a strange thudding sound interrupted everything.

"What was that?" Fortunata jumped to her feet.

Birds cried and flew to the highest treetops. A few small woodland creatures scurried away from the house. Merritt dropped to his knees then turned to look for the source of the sound. He was horrified to see Cillian lying dead on his back, all four legs stiff and pointing up into the air.

* * * *

A pair of dark-eyed faces peered down at him and Denny sputtered as a flurry of hands doused him with a bucket of sea water. Sun and salt smacked his eyes, making him close them again.

"Is he awake?" an anxious male voice asked.

"Let's try it one more time," another man responded. Again they doused Denny with the last thing he wanted in his face. More yucky sea water. It always made his wings sticky and impossible to unstick.

"Enough!" he shrieked, dropping the telescope, which was one of only two weapons he had. He felt for his knife. Gone. One of the men snatched up the telescope before Denny could reach it, and pushed at Denny with his foot. Denny coughed. The water tasted foul. What the heck was in it?

"Is it true?" one of them asked as Denny coughed and spat out the rancid-tasting water.

A tall, dark and very thin man stood poised with a third bucket, and Denny croaked, "You hit me with that and I'll kill you."

The man lowered the bucket but didn't move away from him.

"Is it true?" another man close to Denny asked again,

hunkering down beside him.

"Is what true?" Denny tried sitting. His head hurt like a mother and he gingerly felt the top of it. He was shocked to realize his scalp was covered in egg-like bumps. How many times had Rigby thunked Denny to keep him sleeping in his cabin? How much time had passed since he'd earned his dreaded fairy wings?

"What's the date?" he asked.

"December fifteenth," the man with the bucket said.

"December fifteenth?" Denny repeated. His mouth felt rubbery. He'd been holed up in his quarters for longer than he'd thought. Five months, not three.

"Would you like a cup of coffee?" the bucket man asked.

"I would love one," Denny said, then winced, expecting them all to laugh and jeer at him. He was making such an ass of himself these days.

"Would you like porridge? I can get some for you." The man set the bucket on the deck beside Denny. He peered into it, relieved to see that it wasn't a slop bucket, or somebody's chamber pot. No telltale turds were doing the backstroke on the surface.

"Are you teasing me?" Denny asked.

"Of course not. I'll bring you some right now."

As the man hurried away, Denny wondered if he were dreaming. No. If he were dreaming he'd be back with his tethered prince.

The two remaining men helped Denny to his feet. One of his boots had a wonky heel thanks to his collision with the deck of the La-Di-Da. He could not bring himself to think of it as The Pirate Fairy. He kept stumbling thanks to the stupid heel but he gripped the rail and forced himself to watch his beloved ship sailing away from him. His entire life was on that vessel, including cash and jewels he'd hidden. He was grateful now for the gold he'd stashed in secret places on different islands. Oh, and then there was the house he'd purchased. That seemed farther away than ever now.

"Where are we?" he asked at last, surprised that he could hear music and laughter drifting across the breeze to him from his stolen ship. What the heck was going on over there? Did his crew hate him so much that they were having a farewell party?

"Here you are, sir." The tall, thin man was back with a cup of coffee and a bowl of porridge.

He just called me sir. Maybe I'm dreaming. What a hateful dream, though. Denny squinted up at the guy. "I know you," he said, trying to place him.

The man beamed. "Yes, sir. I'm Ebba. You saved me from the blackbirding ship heading to Peru."

Denny rifled his memory banks. The absinthe had really done a number on him. He couldn't remember very much at all.

"The *Honor*, right?" Denny asked.

"Exactly."

"You worked in my kitchen."

Ebba nodded. "You paid me. And my brother."

"Your name is Ebba?" Denny took the coffee, sniffed, then took a sip of it. "Isn't that a woman's name?"

Ebba's face darkened. "I *am* a woman," she said.

Oops. "Right, right. Sorry. My mind's a muddle. Still can't see straight." *You're the homeliest one I've ever seen. How did I not notice this sooner?*

"That's okay," Ebba kindly said.

Denny looked around at the many faces watching him. Up close nobody seemed ill. They all seemed normal. Happy, even. A few were thin and a bit frail, but the deck was clean of blood and vomit, unlike some blackbirding boats he'd attacked.

Things started coming back to Denny. "Ebba, ah, what about your brother, Larks?" Denny remembered *his* name all right. He couldn't believe he was getting excited thinking about that delectable young man when he was in the middle of possibly the worst catastrophe of his life. Denny felt he could allow himself a small moment of erotic

25

rhapsody. After all, things couldn't be too bad if Ebba was calling him sir and bringing him food and coffee. The coffee was pretty tasty but had a little too much chicory for his taste. He seemed to remember Ebba had a zeal for the stuff, like a lot of Pacific Islanders. He stared at the bowl of porridge she still held for him and noticed the bits of black stuff studding the congealed blob.

"They're currants, right? Or raisins?"

She gave him an odd look. "If it helps you sleep nights to think so, go ahead."

"Meaning they're not?"

"No. They are not."

"I'll stick with coffee then."

"You used to eat my porridge when you thought it had raisins in it." Ebba shrugged.

"Gah!" Denny clutched his throat with his free hand.

"Don't worry. One man's poison is another man's or woman's feast. Rat droppings are pure protein."

Denny thought he might be violently ill as Ebba handed the bowl to a very pregnant woman. She picked out the tiny turds with her long fingers, flicked them overboard then spooned the rest of the bowl's contents into her mouth. She was skinny and frantic-looking, poor thing.

"Hurry," Ebba said to the woman. "We're almost at the port." She looked over her shoulder, throwing a distracted look back toward Denny. "Hide the gold Captain Rigby gave us for him."

"Captain Rigby?" Denny almost choked on his coffee.

They all stared at him.

"But he's my second mate." He glanced around him. There was something very odd about all of this. "What's going on?" he asked, almost falling to the deck thanks to his broken heel.

Ebba pulled a face. "Don't worry. You won't be sold into slavery until after the trial."

He gaped at her. "What do you mean slavery? And what trial?"

26

"You'll soon be on trial for your life."

"I will? Why?"

She squinted at him. "You're a pirate!"

"But I was good to you, wasn't I?" he whined. *Please, God, or whoever else is up there, please tell me I was good to her.* He braced himself for bad news, but Ebba gave him a sweet smile. Man, she was ugly! Many of the people on board looked strange, with misshapen heads, crossed eyes, drooping ears, extra-long fingers, and, he realized, the oddest feet he'd ever seen. Some of them looked elongated and resembled talons.

"You were very good to me, sir. You employed me and gave me dignity and courage. You let me leave your ship and join the one heading to the Canary Islands."

Denny tore his gaze away from the myriad webbed feet and bobbed his head up and down for lack of a response. He had no clue what she was talking about. He was beginning to feel ill and wondered if there was something fishy in his coffee.

Ebba took the cup from his hands. "Your kindness is the only reason you haven't been kept in shackles since we took you aboard. I wanted to show you respect where it was due."

"Eh? What's that?" he asked. His throat had gone dry. "You mean this isn't a slave ship?"

"Of course it is, but not the kind you're thinking of," Ebba said. "We are all liberated slaves and we travel the seas hunting those who hurt us. We lead them to justice."

"And what am *I* doing here?"

"Facing justice, just like all the others."

"But I—"

"No, no." She held up a hand. "I'm not interested in what you have to say. You'll have a chance to defend your actions with the jury. And now, sir, I'm very sorry, but I must put you in arm and leg restraints before we leave the ship. The court demands it."

"What court is this?" Denny asked as they neared the

27

coast. He wanted to scream when Ebba took one of his hands and snapped a shackle onto his wrist. Over her head, a huge palace loomed far off in the distance up a mountain. It sparkled like a pale blue and lavender jewel. Its winding staircase twinkled under the sun's rays. It was so very inviting, and he felt encouraged until he saw several men in handcuffs and stocks near the coastline. They all looked depressed. Some of them had suffered beatings, judging by their bleeding lips and dark bruises.

I've got to get my wings to work. If I can just get them to flap I can fly away. To his detriment, he realized he'd spent so much time pretending he didn't have wings and railing against the damned things that he still didn't know how to make them work.

As the ship drifted toward the harbor, a host of canoes traveled across the small ripples of sea water to greet them.

"Where are we?" he asked Ebba. He'd never seen such odd-looking creatures as those preparing to storm the boat. Denny almost wished his crew had tied cannonballs to his feet and made him walk the plank.

The men preparing to board the vessel all had wings. Some looked like pretty, gossamer fairies, others looked like giant birds of prey.

"This is the Kingdom of Aramann," Ebba said. "Today you will face your destiny."

"But you said I was good to you," Denny whimpered.

"Yeah. You were. But you were horrible to my brother. You made him your sexual partner and when he finally said you'd had enough of him, you—"

"Ebba!" a voice called out.

Ebba turned, waving to the young man paddling a canoe. Denny recognized him and inwardly cringed. It was Larks. Larks, who had felt tremendous guilt enjoying sex with another man and who had carried his shame around like a stuffed carpet bag. Larks had refused Denny in the end. Denny had forced him to choose. Either he caved into the inevitable, or he'd walk the plank. To this moment, Denny

28

recalled the way Larks had chosen the plank and had swum away laughing. So, this was how he'd wound up. Leading the charge to drag prisoners off to trials.

Date with Destiny. I am going to survive this so I can find that bastard Rigby and make him pay for this.

I'm a sitting duck. Larks knew of the murdering and marauding on the high seas. Denny was the one who had forced him to walk the plank, which most men did not survive. Denny was forced to submit to being chained from ankle to neck and wondered how he would survive any type of trial.

Larks knew too much about him. And clearly hated him.

"Somebody else take the pirate fairy," Larks announced to the men lined up in canoes. "If I'm left alone with him I might make *him* walk the plank, and I want to see justice served." He looked up at Denny, revulsion in his gaze.

Denny tried to keep his expression neutral, even as he noticed the fear and panic among the bound and blindfolded men ashore.

None of us will get out of here alive. Not a single sodding one of us.

His tormentors forced Denny from the ship and pushed him into the water. Unable to move his hands or legs, he almost sank to the bottom, except that strong hands reached for him.

"No," Larks said. "Drowning's too quick, too easy for you. I think you need to be sodomized by eight men. But you might like that, knowing you." He glanced down and shook his head when he saw Denny's tented trousers. "You dirty sod, you."

29

Chapter Three

Merritt panicked. He crawled around the side of the house, his heart thundering so loudly he was certain both Gremma and Fortunata would hear him. He hid underneath the fronds of a dense fern, catching snatches of their conversation. He didn't know what to think as Fortunata railed about the dead horse.

"How am I supposed to get back to the palace now? Walk?" she screeched. His sister's long, curly blonde hair cascaded down her back. For two people who were twins, she and Merritt couldn't have been more different. Though her face was beautiful, her black heart constantly surprised him. And yet, she was capable of goodness and that was why he'd never given up on her.

"I don't know, my lady. Look at this poor creature's face. He died an agonizing death."

"So what? I can't walk all the way back."

Typical Fortunata. Thinks of nothing but herself.

"My lady, the horse appears poisoned." Gremma sounded petrified.

"Well, he ate the wrong grass. Stupid animal."

"But there is nothing here that would ever harm an animal. I would never—"

"*You* do not have dominion over this kingdom. *I* do." Fortunata's imperious tone had Merritt rolling his eyes. He was angry now. It was obvious that his trusted Elvin was a snake in elf's clothing.

He tried to kill me. I can never go back to the palace. I've been so stupid. I let my grief overpower me and I let her use my powers. Without them, she is nothing. She needs me, and I need her. Damn it. I haven't exercised my powers in so long because I believed Denny was safe. But he isn't. She says he's marked for death.

A light rain fell, and he huddled under the fern's massive leaves. Fortunata and Gremma continued their strange discussion. It was harder to hear in the rain, but the good thing was it also disguised his sharp breathing and any slight noise he might make. The two women walked toward the forest. He held his breath as he caught a glimpse of Fortunata's swishing, burgundy-colored gown. Gremma seemed dressed in rags.

Why does such a powerful witch dress like that? And why doesn't she do something about her hands and hair?

He crawled to the side of the house once more and listened. No sound of female voices. He stood and made his way to the front door, but when he turned the handle, it wouldn't open. How frustrating. He peered through the open windows, pushing aside the lace fabric over the biggest one on the other side of the house. He was astonished to see an altar above the fireplace. Upon it was a gold chain Merritt recognized as his own. Beside it was a black candle smeared with red liquid. Blood. Beside it was a pair of shoes, also his own. Filled with wide beeswax candles that had almost burned down, covering the soft leather moccasins with wax.

My God. She's put a spell on me. Once that wax burns down, she'll have complete control of me.

How had he not realized earlier that his sister was working against him? She must have figured out that Elvin was following her. Perhaps he had been under her sway all the time. Had he knowingly given Merritt the poisoned apple? His thoughts swirled and he panicked as he gazed at the other objects on the altar.

Why is Fortunata trying to kill me? If she destroys me, she loses half her magic.

He no longer cared if she or Gremma returned. He climbed through the window into the cottage and moved toward the altar. Tiny needles dug into his feet and ankles.

31

He glanced down at the writhing mass of black snakes, conjured by magic. He'd never been so angry in his life.

"Let go of me," he muttered and flicked his hand at them.

The snakes disappeared. A small ginger cat stared at him fearfully from a hole in the wall. Obviously the poor creature had been too afraid to come out with the snakes on the floor.

My sister and cousin were expecting me. He pushed back his sleeves and moved to the altar. No, perhaps not. Gremma is working spells on many people. He could see that now. Little piles of hair, jewels, clothing. It was all frightening and horrible. He grabbed what he could, including a lock of black hair he was certain belonged to Denny, and stuffed everything in his pockets. The black candle was definitely smeared in blood. He could tell by the smell.

But whose?

He grabbed that too, and made for the window once again, but somebody was at the door. The handle turned and it creaked open.

My God. Too late.

* * * *

Denny joined the others on the shore. It was so hot his clothes dried pretty fast, but the seawater smelled foul.

"Polluted waters," a man who stood beside Denny told him. "Don't judge this book by its cover. The palace and court look like something out of a fairytale but nobody here seems to have heard of hygiene."

Denny didn't have time to respond. A man with massive black wings flapping approached him. "Pirate?"

"Um, yeah."

The man gazed at Denny's coat. "No use hiding those wings here. How adept are you with them?"

"Not adept at all."

The man looked surprised. "You haven't learned how to use them?"

"No. They hurt."

"That's because you don't work with them." The black-winged man gave him a disapproving look. "Not that you could fly away from here anyway."

Denny wanted to shrug but his whole body ached. Adrenaline had surged and spent itself in his body. He wished he were back in his cabin dreaming. Captain Rigby would take it over. *Ha ha! Hope he likes dirty sheets. Gulp. Wonder if he'll find my stash of gold?*

"Did they tell you what charges you face?" The black-winged man glanced up at Denny from a large notebook in his hand.

"No, they didn't."

"Did they say anything?"

"They said I was on trial for my life."

"Ah." The man nodded, a knowing look on his face. "That's a capital punishment case. Take the line over here to the right."

Denny shuffled away and the black-winged man shouted at him, "Quickly. You think you have all day?"

"I'm doing my best. My feet are chained."

"Why did they do that?"

"They said the court demanded it."

"Not usually. Well, get a move on. Some of us have homes to get to before dark."

Denny shuffled on, each step making his legs and ankles twinge in pain. He almost fell, and when he steadied himself, blood trickled down his left wrist.

Oh, spiffing! This is exactly what I wanted to do today. Get beaten up, shackled, and go on trial for a capital crime!

"Plunder and pillage?" a man with green wings asked him.

"Pillage before plunder," Denny responded.

The man quirked an eyebrow at him.

"Sorry. I'm a pirate. I can't help wanting things in order." He cringed at the man's fierce expression.

"So you admit to piracy."

"Well, yeah. Of course." *Not much point in denying it.*

"Do you have use of your wings?"

"No."

"That's what they all say. Take off your coat."

"I can't."

"They all say that, too." The green-winged head case seemed aware only then that Denny was bound by a rusted metal collar, chains and arm and leg restraints. "Oh." He looked around. "Where is his public defender?"

"Er, she's washing dishes," came back a tiny woman's voice.

Denny looked down to see a dainty fairy fluttering around his feet. Denny felt more depressed than ever. Only he could have a public defender who also washed dishes for a living. He tried to act nonchalant but all of a sudden he had a desperate urge to pee. He understood now why the other prisoner had mentioned the island's poor hygiene. Men in chains were making their way down to the shoreline and peeing right into the water. *Lovely.*

Denny's spirits lifted a little when Ebba approached him. She'd changed into a red and white floral dress. Denny couldn't believe it. He'd seen men dressed as women before but she looked worse than any of them. She was a man. He was certain of it. She also wore a hat covered in what looked like fresh strawberries. And she was barefoot. Ebba spotted Denny, smiled and gave him a wave.

"Howdy do," she said to Denny as though they were meeting at some barn dance and not for his date with bloody destiny.

"Yeah. Howdy," he griped.

"Unshackle him," the green-winged man said.

"Yes, sir." Ebba fumbled in her pocket for a set of keys. Once she'd produced it, she worked the lock on his collar. Her hands were shaking.

"You're my public defender?" he asked.

Her hands stopped moving. "Yes." She turned the key again.

The lock was rusty but it eventually gave way and the collar loosened around his neck. The release of pressure put him in a better mood within seconds. As the rest of his restraints fell away, Denny believed for one small moment that he could escape all of this.

But where would I go? How do I get away?

Ebba removed his coat and everyone stared as his slightly bent, gossamer fairy wings came into view.

"Okay, show me what you can do." The green-winged man poked at his chest. Now that Denny no longer wore the cloak, his wings pained him more than ever. He let out a gasp.

"What's the matter with you?" Ebba asked.

"They hurt. No. Hurt's not enough. They're bloody agony." Tears sparked in Denny's eyes.

Both Ebba and the green-winged man stared at him, then at each other.

"You've got a crybaby for a client," the green-winged man said. "He's full of it." He stared at Denny. "Make them flap or I'll do it for you."

"I don't know how," Denny whined. Boy, he was sure doing a lot of that lately.

"Try."

"How do I do it? Do I speak to them? Do I move my shoulders or something?" Denny's desperate gaze flicked from side to side.

"You just do it." The green-winged man reached over and grabbed one of the wings. Denny's ear-piercing shrieks made several people drop to the ground, ducking for cover, as though somebody was shooting indiscriminately in the crowd.

"Blimey!" the green-winged man said. "You weren't kidding. Your wings are stuck!"

Denny had dropped to his knees and panted in pain. Tears streaked down his face. "Thank you. This happened to me five months ago and I've had nobody to talk to. They hurt every day."

35

The green-winged man moved behind Denny and knelt, studying the wings a little closer. He poked at the feathers and slid his hand underneath Denny's slitted shirt. He touched a particularly tender spot on Denny's right shoulder blade. It hurt, but Denny found that the man's prodding sent a mixture of pleasure and pain down his back, so he just breathed through the worst moments. "This one's atrophied a bit. It's clear you haven't used them, which contravenes our rules for judgment here. You might have to be sent to a different court."

A harsh gasp shot out throughout the assembled throng. Denny looked up to see Ebba's horrified expression. She shook her head at him then uttered an emphatic, "No. He's still one of us. He still counts. He was cursed and it's clear that something went wrong. Can you imagine how much pain he's been in?"

The green-winged man didn't respond.

"She said she'd turned the fairy into a fairy," Denny said, desperation pouring from his very soul.

A hushed silence fell over them all.

"Who did this to you?" The green-winged man got to his feet once more.

Denny fought the urge to purge all over the ground. He gulped in air and was about to mutter her name but caught Ebba's slight shake of her head. "I don't know her name."

The green-winged man looked suspicious. "So this woman cursed you for no good reason?"

"I rejected her." Denny didn't look at Ebba in case she was shaking her head again.

"She wanted you for a lover?" The green-winged man looked surprised.

"I'm an attractive man, or I was." Denny hung his head. He had mad urges to barf and cry. Never in his life had he felt so helpless or ashamed. Not since he'd been a kid.

"Whatever helps you sleep nights," Ebba murmured. Now why did she keep saying that to him? First it was his belief that his porridge had fruit in it. Now it was his looks.

What the hell did that bitch Fortunata do to me? His hands flew to his face. He was hairier than he remembered but everything else seemed to be the same. No hooked nose or hair-sprouting moles from what he could tell.

For the first time in weeks, he allowed himself to think about Prince Merritt and Princess Fortunata. How could two siblings be so very different? One so good and loving, the other so diabolical? It struck him for the first time that they were so much like Denny and his sister, Polly, that it was almost frightening.

"Get up," Ebba said, hauling Denny to his feet. His face mashed into her boobies. Boobies. She *was* a girl. He had a sudden hunch that she, like he, had been cursed. He looked at her as he wobbled on his broken boot heel.

"Why are you looking at me that way?" she snapped. "Stop crying. Nobody likes a sniveling pirate."

"Under the circumstances, he can be tried in the fairy court," the green-winged man muttered. "He is a fairy, even though his wings are buggered up." He wrote something in his notebook. "I will refrain from making an official notification about your handicap. I'll give you time to work on your wings." He pointed to his left. "I'm doing this for Ebba, so do not waste this opportunity. She knows the way."

Indeed she did. She led Denny to a path away from the shoreline. Things smelled a bit better here. Denny took a deep breath.

"It's okay here now," Ebba said. "The holding cells are quite pleasant. They'll bring you something to eat and you can wash. I'll see what I can do about your boots. You're falling all over the place. We don't want them thinking you're the sad old drunk we both know you really are."

"Hey! I'm not old. I'm twenty-five!"

"Okay. You're a sad drunk then."

"Hey! I'm not sad, or a drunk."

"Hey, yourself. Have you looked in a mirror lately? You look like crap. Alcohol has aged you and don't tell me you're

37

not a drunk. You don't even remember what happened to me, do you?"

He gulped. "Nope."

"I tried to protect you when Fortunata cursed you."

"You did?" It was all so hazy. He'd been so horrified when the pretty princess had turned herself into an ugly old crone he recalled nothing else.

"I stood right in front of you. Because I protected you, she got mad. I protected a fairy so she turned me into a...a... girly man."

"Oh, my God. I am so sorry." Denny clutched Ebba's arms.

She shrugged him off. "No big thing. I like being both. I have my male parts and my female parts. I'm officially recognized as a woman, but there are men who like both." She suddenly smiled. "I give them the best of both worlds. My two husbands can testify to that." She pushed him through the side entrance of a black and white marble building.

"This is the court?" Denny looked around.

"Yes. The Supernatural Superior Court. You are not on the Code Red list. Yet. You won't face the judge or jury until tomorrow. In the meantime, get some rest. I'll see if I can't get someone in here to give you a shave. You look like a crazy hermit right now." She left him at a check-in counter where a man who looked like a human bumblebee with huge, thick glasses waited for him.

"And practice using your feathers," Ebba muttered in Denny's ears. "There are two fairies on the jury. They won't take kindly to you weeping about your wings. I'll be back tonight. We need to prepare your defense."

Denny hated to see her leave, but the bumblebee was talking to him. Denny strained to hear him. It wasn't easy since every word out of the man's mouth was accompanied by some serious buzzing. Denny listened as the man told him he would be held pending his piracy trial. "You'll be in Cell Block D. That's a nice one. They give you blankets in there."

"Okay, thanks." Denny kept hoping he was having a bad dream, but soon he was heading to his cell, a few men ahead of him. One guy was half eagle, half man. He had only one wing. His jealous glance in Denny's direction made Denny feel ashamed for having made such a fuss about *two* wings. With two wings he could do something. With one wing, oh, boy. That would have been cruel. And here was a man living with it.

Denny followed the bumblebee man into a bare-walled cell that had a window protected by frosted glass and tiny, thick bars. He couldn't see out, but light streamed in. He had a narrow bed with a pillow and blankets piled on one end. A small table and chair had been pushed against the wall. The bumblebee man hung a mirror on a hook nailed into the wall above it. Denny needed to get a look at himself. How bad was he? But the chamber pot beckoned and as soon as the cell door locked behind the bumblebee man, Denny made use of the pot, covering it with a cloth tucked into the handle.

A man without wings but the head of a fox and tail to match came in with a large pot of steaming water. He wore ordinary clothes, his tail protruding from the back of his pants. "I understand you have a wing problem."

Denny nodded.

"Take everything off."

Denny didn't mind if he did. He stood naked as the fox man looked him over then placed the basin on the table. He beckoned Denny over to him. Using a gigantic sea sponge, he cleaned Denny's face. Denny inhaled the fragrance of the scented water. Roses and lavender. He almost swooned. The fox man went over Denny's entire feathers.

"You have to keep these clean. Your feathers have been stuck for some time. Looks and feels like candle wax. Did you fall into a lit candle or something?"

Denny was about to say no, but from somewhere deep in his memory banks, he recalled a late-night brawl. He seemed to remember being pushed against a wall beneath a candle sconce. When had that happened? Had he been injured? "Maybe," he admitted.

The man gave him a kind smile. "Unless you use your wings, you'll forget your human life. You'll remember things from long ago but not recent activities. Your body is rejecting the fairy experience, but you belong to both worlds now."

"What happened to you?" Denny asked.

The fox man stopped sponging Denny's wings. "I was cursed." He sighed and began dabbing again. "I rejected the crown princess."

Denny's heart sank. "What was her name?"

The fox man's hand shook. "Fortunata."

Denny stiffened.

The fox man put a steadying hand on Denny's very sore wing. His voice dropped to a whisper. "Don't you know that's why you're here?"

"No. I know nothing. My crew mutinied against me and here I am."

"Lucky for you. I read your case notes. Ebba paid gold for your recovery."

"But I thought my crew gave her gold to take me."

"Ha! They did. But she paid gold to informants to find your ship. We've been tracking you for weeks. If she gives a good defense of you, she can have her curse reversed."

"Can I?"

"Don't be stupid. You'll be lucky if you're sentenced to slavery. Most pirates are sentenced to death."

"I still don't understand why I'm here." It hurt to think that Ebba had been looking out for herself all this time. He'd wanted to believe that he had a chance to make it out alive.

"Keep your voice down." The fox man squeezed the sponge into the now very black water and patted Denny's bad wing again. "Princess Fortunata is being held captive on a ship. Nobody knows where. But in her absence, the prince—"

"Merritt?" Denny asked excitedly.

"Yes, Prince Merritt. Do you know him?"

"Very well." *Intimately. You might say biblically.*

The fox man frowned. "I wouldn't admit that to anybody else if I were you. I'm telling you all of this in confidence. Shall I continue?"

"Yes. Please do."

"He's holding these trials, trying to figure out where she is. It was always rumored that you were the one who took her captive, though it's obvious since you haven't harnessed your magical powers that it's impossible that you have her. I hear the prince is not happy."

"I have magical powers?"

"Of course. Were you always this stupid or is it only since you became a fairy?"

"What sort of magical powers?" Denny was incensed that he'd known none of this and that he'd wallowed in self-pity all this time.

"You can fly. You can't die from a gunshot wound. You can see things humans can't. When you harness your power, you have acute hearing and vision. And for a male fairy, your dick gets huge. I mean really huge."

This day was suddenly getting better. Denny absorbed all of this. He recalled letting the prince go because Merritt had confessed that their mutual love would affect his kingdom and his ability to rule. He was supposed to marry a woman and had been promised to a rival royal family's daughter. Fortunata had refused to leave the ship, not suspecting her brother's relationship with Denny. Well, that's what she'd said at first, but Denny had been honest and it turned out she had known all along and blamed Denny for her brother's sexual deviation.

He'd been truthful about everything and paid the price for it. Was it too late for him to explore his new power and use it to his advantage?

"If I can't die by gunshot, how do fairies die?" Denny

asked.

The fox man looked at him. "You should live forever, unless you ingest poison, or—"He paused dramatically. "You drink to excess. Each alcoholic beverage shortens your lifespan by a year."

Denny's mind went into a spiral of shock, denial, anger then acceptance. He'd stop drinking from now on. He resented that his crew had given him endless bottles of absinthe and wine. *They were trying to get me to die!*

"What is your name?" Denny asked the fox man, who rubbed at a waxy spot on Denny's wing."

"Barthelmass."

"Nice name."

"Thank you. And what about your curse? Can they lift it?"

Barthelmass moved in front of Denny and looked at him. "No. I never asked. I don't feel cursed. I feel blessed. I can outrun any man I know. I have sharp senses of smell and hearing and I have plenty of girlfriends." He smiled. "At least I did, until I met the love of my life and wanted to get married. According to the Supernatural Superior Court, we can't do that until one of us has our curse removed."

"Oh, that's so sad."

"We're considered mixed races now." Barthelmass looked devastated but recovered quickly. He moved behind Denny again and rubbed at the wing. It hurt, but Denny didn't say so.

"There," Barthelmass said. "Your wing is clear. Try to keep them free of restriction as much as possible. I'll finish bathing you. See if you can't get them to flap."

"How do I do that? Everybody keeps telling me to try without telling me how to do it."

"Imagine them flapping. I didn't know what to do with my fox tail when I got it. Had some nasty bathroom accidents at first, which the ladies didn't find so sexy."

"No. I imagine not."

Barthelmass squeezed the sponge into the water again

42

and pressed Denny's skin. The pain of the wax-glugged wing had subsided, and having another man touch his bare skin made his cock go *boing*. *Uh-oh*. He had to stop that.

"Imagine you have always had them. Picture them flapping. Send a message to them. Ask them to flap for you. To show you their magic."

Denny did as he'd been told. Nothing happened at first. For several long minutes, he agonized over the futility of his efforts, but Barthelmass kept saying encouraging things.

"Feel their power. Persuade them back into life. Wings have feelings, too." Barthelmass moved in front of Denny, washing his throat and chest. He teased Denny's nipples with a moist fingertip as well as a gentle swipe of the sponge.

Denny could no longer hide his boner, and Barthelmass didn't seem to take offense. In fact he captured Denny's massive cock in his hand and stroked it. "Feel your power," he coaxed. "Show me your wings!" Barthelmass stroked Denny's cock with increasing force.

This seemed to set off a series of intense feelings deep within Denny's body. The orgasm he had at the hands of the fox man made Denny's wings twitch.

"That's it." The fox man kept his grip on Denny's cock with one hand, the other touching the feathers in Denny's wings. The wings vibrated.

"You're doing it."

Denny's feet left the ground, but Barthelmass brought him back again. "I opened you up," he said, "but now you'll have to learn to do it without somebody bringing you sexual release."

"Okay," Denny said, hugely disappointed that it was over. He wanted so much more with the fox man.

Barthelmass finished cleaning Denny then handed him a pair of cotton pants and a shirt that gave the wings in his back freedom of movement.

Denny was confused about many things, such as why he needed his wings to work, but suddenly it came to

43

him. Orgasm had released months of cloudy thoughts and feelings. Denny needed to show the court that he had accepted his new condition. That he harbored no ill feeling toward the princess. Even though he did.

The cotton pants he slid up and over his thighs reminded him of another jail in another time and place in a galaxy far, far away. He trotted to the bed and lay on his side.

"That's good." Barthelmass used the same gentle, coaxing tone he had earlier. "Rest now. And start again as soon as you're awake."

"You're lovely to me." Denny sighed when Barthelmass ran a cool hand over Denny's brow.

"Ebba is the woman I want to be my wife. I want her to be free," Barthelmass said. "She is the best thing in my life. She has explored both sides of her sexuality and if she becomes solely a woman, the laws will allow us to be married." He picked up the basin and left.

Denny was too spent to even say goodbye. He fell into a deep sleep. He had always gravitated toward men but had no idea of how to pursue his desire for sexual contact with another. He'd gotten the chance unexpectedly when he was eighteen and thrown into a Spanish jail during a stop at the sea port of Tarragona, in the Mediterranean Sea. Denny had taken to sea life with remarkable ease and had been so influenced by his superior officers when they'd gone astray that he'd joined them on their less savory antics. Particularly when it had involved drinking. Though Denny chafed at authority, he shone when a superior officer befriended him. It came from his years as a street urchin. Always desperate to belong, he'd trotted beside the ship's crewmembers when they'd stepped away from hauling barrels onto the ship and slipped into one of the many tavernas dotting the port.

For the first time, Denny had tasted the local drink, Chartreuse, an extremely alcoholic green drink that tasted sweet at first, but then developed a strong and pungent aftertaste that made the drinker imbibe more to get back

44

the sweetness. Denny and the crew had ordered platters of *pa amb tomàquet*, which had turned out to be large slices of square toasted bread with scrapings of tomato laced with olive oil and salt. Denny couldn't believe how good such a simple meal could taste. He thought of the numerous nights he and his sister, Polly, had slept without food in their bellies. Like the others, he'd kept drinking.

It had been something of a shock to find himself on a stone floor the next morning inside a jail cell. The place had been noisy and the head jailer had come to see him when a guard had alerted him that their prisoner was awake.

"Where are the others?" Denny had asked, sitting up and wishing the world would stop spinning.

The head jailer had paced. "My name is Christoph and I oversee things here."

Denny had panicked that he'd been left behind, and waited for the news.

"Your friends refused to pay their bill and your captain, Lester Piggins, will not pay for it. He says he will leave you all here until you've learned your lesson."

Denny had hated the sound of that and had plotted against Piggins from that moment.

"I understand," Denny had said. What else could he have said? He didn't speak Spanish and he'd been at the mercy of this Christoph guy who, though not especially attractive, had had a seductive accent, and so far had seemed quite kind.

Christoph had left him alone then, and for hours and hours, Denny had remained that way in his cell. He'd had no idea what was going on but had heard occasional chatter from other prisoners scattered around him. He'd tried to peer out of the bars of his cell, but hadn't been able to see much. A frantic urge to pee had left him disheartened when he'd noticed the slop bucket in the corner. He'd made use of it, but it had demoralized him.

He'd done nothing wrong, or had he?

Chapter Four

Merritt somehow made it out of the window, but dropped one of the items he'd stuffed down his shirt. Damn. It was the black candle. Gremma could still use it to work magic against the person whose blood had touched it.

"No!" she yelled as he dropped back inside and grabbed it, but Merritt made his way out of the window again and took off running. She followed him, but he lost her. He ran and he ran, hiding far in the forest. Her voice followed him until he climbed higher up into the dense forest and found a small cave. Once he was sure he was alone, he sat just inside the entrance. He took out everything, including the sandwich that might or might not have been poisoned. He was starving now and the sky grew dark. He'd been gone all day. His sister would be frantic, no doubt, but he didn't care. He examined all the objects he was certain had been stolen from unluckily hexed victims. Psychometry had been his gift until he and Fortunata had had the misfortune of being abducted. Neither of them had been able to harness their power because Merritt had been shackled. Then Denny had come to their rescue.

He wouldn't think about that now. He had to find out who had owned each object before him and return the items in order to break the spell Fortunata had over them. He moved his hand over everything. He'd start with the sandwich. It was the most recent object that had possibly been hexed.

Merritt's magic was strong but he'd declined to use it all these months because nothing mattered to him without Denny. He'd allowed Fortunata such power while in his

46

depressed state that he now realized this new-found power had gone to her head. Well, not anymore. He touched the sandwich, closed his eyes and willed his head to empty itself of all thoughts. Nothing came at first then he saw the faint light in the corner of his mind. No matter how hard he tried, the image remained blurry.

Concentrate.

His head pounded and he opened his eyes, looking down at his fingertips. They were black. He'd absorbed magic from somewhere. Was it the sandwich? He looked beside it. The candle. Whose blood was it? He knew he needed to release the negative energy in his hands before he could work on the candle. The only thing that could release such dark magic was love. True love. Merritt closed his eyes again, and Denny's face was right there. Merritt's heart almost broke remembering how they had come to know each other. The stolen kisses, the furtive touching and hand-holding. He'd loved taming the fierce pirate of the high seas just by loving him.

Merritt smiled, remembering how he was the one who'd planned Denny's seduction in a rented room in Tarragona, a busy sea port in Spain. Denny had some weird history with the place, that Merritt still didn't understand but suspected it had something to do with a man. He'd sent a message to Denny, who'd come to meet him. Freshly shaved and washed, he'd smelled divine. They'd shared frantic kisses, Merritt touching Denny's crotch. He had delighted at the thick, hard cock eager for his touch. Merritt knew that Denny's tastes were a bit kinky. Not by anything Denny had said, but by the occasional snatches of memory Merritt had gleaned from him.

Just as he was getting to the good part of his reverie where he sucked Denny's cock, another image shifted into his mind. Fortunata shimmered into view, then Gremma. Then he saw the horse. Poor, dear Cillian. Merritt gasped. He glimpsed Elvin in the palace kitchens assembling the package of food he'd given Merritt earlier that day. One of the kitchen maids was in there scrubbing vegetables and she chided him for ransacking the food stocks.

"It's for the prince," he said, his voice sounding loud in Merritt's mind.

"Ah, well, if it's for him, then that's okay. Give him an apple. He loves those. Especially the green ones."

Elvin smiled and plucked one from the bowl. He wrapped the package and went to Merritt's bedroom. The image shifted just as Elvin opened the door.

The food wasn't poisoned. I don't think it was the apple.

Merritt's eyes flew open as a flash of pain hit him right in the side. It was as though somebody had stuck him with a knife.

He fell over on the cave floor, panting, sweat beading on his head.

In his agony, he reached for the black candle. Instantly, the image of Fortunata cutting Cillian's shoulder with a small, pointed blade flew into his mind. She laughed as Cillian whinnied and reared. The horse took off and she ran back to Gremma's house, smearing the candle with the horse's blood.

"What are you doing?" Gremma asked. "Who have you cursed now?" She paused then waved her hand over the altar. "Isn't this enough? Haven't you done enough now?" Gremma looked horrified. "You hate your brother that much?"

"No. I love his power that much. His pirate lover will soon be here, and I'll get rid of him, too." She threw back her head and unleashed a wild cackle that left Merritt shaking in the dark cave.

* * * *

Denny dreamed of Tarragona and his life in the cell there. He felt as though he had gone back in time and relived the moment he fell asleep sitting against the wall there. Somehow, he'd gotten through a rough night filled with

48

strange noises, weird smells and severe hunger pangs.

* * * *

Tarragona

A few years earlier…
The morning after his captain had left them, a jailer brought him a cup of coffee and a hunk of warm bread. That was when his love affair with coffee began.

Christoph came and talked to him, his heavily accented English quite charming to Denny, who was beside himself with happiness when a second cup of coffee and another hunk of bread came his way in the afternoon. Late in the evening, a jailer came to collect him.

Denny had lost all sense of time but knew it was night because lit candles highlighted a narrow, pebbled corridor that led away from the cells. A hand snatched at him from between two bars. *Rigby.* The man that Denny would later make his second mate.

"We knew he liked you best. Let him have his way with you. We've got to get out of here."

"I—"

"No talking!" Christoph boomed from somewhere ahead of Denny and the jailer.

Rigby shrank away from the bars.

The jailer led Denny to a small office that was a far cry from Denny's horrible conditions. A soft sofa where Christoph now sat, eased Denny's cold, aching bones.

"Come. Sit by me." Christoph patted the tan-colored sofa cushion. The jailer gave Denny a lingering, pitying look then left him alone with Christoph.

There was no chit-chat. No warning. "Have you ever experienced another man's touch?" Christoph leaned close to Denny. He'd clearly washed and shaved for the occasion.

Denny blinked, realizing that the head jailer meant to have his way with him. Denny noticed the faint scars crisscrossing the man's face and wondered how he'd gotten

49

them. The predatory gleam in Christoph's gaze scared him.

Will I get out alive?

"*Follemos,*" Christoph whispered. His huge dark eyes held a predatory gleam that seemed to translate the single Spanish word he'd uttered.

Denny didn't understand Spanish but felt certain *follemos* did not mean tennis. Or cards. He had a pretty good idea that Christoph was hungry for sex the way he was rubbing at Denny's trousers, moving his hand upward from knee to groin. His growing frenzy frightened Denny, who held his breath in total terror as Christoph leaned into him, inhaling Denny's sea scent. Denny couldn't remember the last time he'd bathed and was embarrassed by his own smell. Not that Christoph minded. He kept rubbing, moving his probing fingers along the length of Denny's hardening cock.

Denny suddenly didn't mind the way Christoph worked the buttons on Denny's thick wool trousers.

"*Me encanta.*" Christoph moaned as he withdrew Denny's cock from his pants. What did *me encanta* mean?

As though reading his mind, Christoph tore his gaze from Denny's huge cock and said in his thick English, "I love it." Christoph dropped his gaze again, his mouth open in wonderment.

His hot breath sent tantalizing messages to Denny's shaft, which only hardened and lengthened under Christoph's scrutiny. Denny knew he had a big cock. The way Christoph was nattering on about it in his guttural Spanish, Denny suspected Christoph was delirious about Denny's enormous manhood.

Denny was still sitting on the sofa beside Christoph, except he kept arching his body upward, the tip of his erection just an inch from Christoph's mouth. Nobody had ever examined his cock so closely. Christoph seemed mesmerized, no, *fixated* with Denny's engorged cock. No man had looked that way at him before and it did some strange things to his whole body. A tingling sensation began in his groin. Sweat beaded on his lip. His scalp itched.

The back of his head and the nape of his neck dampened. He thought he might be experiencing a flash fever, but then Christoph touched him and Denny's body twitched and bucked in response. He longed to shout, 'Touch me, lick it!' but dared not. This was his captor, but Christoph seemed unaware of this fact as he reached out tentatively and touched Denny's pride.

"Oh!" Denny bit off the words he was desperate to say as Christoph stroked Denny's most private parts. Christoph held Denny's gaze for a moment then grew bolder, clasping the base of Denny's cock in his fist. Christoph glanced up at Denny as his head dipped down, his lips moist.

"*Quérico*," he whispered. "I like this. *So much*." Christoph kept studying Denny's uncut cock then licked his lips.

He gave Denny a seductive grin that made Denny grow even harder. *Oh, no.* His cock was leaking but Christoph looked thrilled. He kissed the head, sending waves of happiness through Denny's body. Christoph stroked Denny harder, faster, exalting in the way Denny's cock arced toward him.

"I need you now," Christoph moaned, plunging Denny's length into his salivating mouth.

Denny fell from the sofa and sank to his knees, Christoph tumbling beside him, keeping his mouth glued to Denny's slick shaft.

Somebody was coming. Footsteps echoed. *Oh no. Not now. Please don't stop.* Denny longed for the carousel in his head to keep spinning. The faint unpleasantness of his unaccustomed, mounting arousal turned out to be a sexual tension Denny had never before experienced. His balls grew tighter, bigger, his cock seeming to bring Christoph's searing lips as much pleasure as Christoph gave to Denny. Then he stopped. His eyes were languid as he released Denny, who almost howled in frustration. Christoph must have sensed it because he gave Denny a wicked, lopsided grin as he dipped his head again and used his tongue and two fingers to peel back Denny's foreskin, revealing the shimmering head.

Christoph claimed Denny's cock once more, sucking him into his mouth then releasing his strong pull, letting Denny slip out of his lips, only to grab him back in again. This constant motion produced an exhilarating sensation from deep within Denny, who began to help, pushing and pulling his shaft in and out of Christoph's mouth. With a sharp cry that Christoph muffled with his free hand, Denny came in Christoph's mouth. He was both in that warm office, feeling Christoph's wayward tongue swirling over his eruption, but also high in the sky.

"Beautiful." Christoph released him. "You liked it?"

"Oh, yes." Denny was desperate to return the favor. "Please let me pleasure you, Christoph."

"Not now. I will send for you again tomorrow and we can enjoy our new friendship then, but for now, you must return to your cell."

Outside the door, the footsteps Denny had heard earlier returned and he was surprised when, for the first time, Christoph kissed Denny on the lips. He tasted his own semen on Christoph's tongue.

"My juices are sweet," he said, surprised at the realization.

"That's because we are not feeding you meat," Christoph said. "Meat makes men's seed so bitter." Denny returned to his cell, alone with his thoughts, his racing pulse and a heightened awareness that he had forever changed.

He lay on his bunk, his stomach rumbling. He'd missed dinner, but had received so much more. The start of his sexual education. He didn't think he could sleep but the carnal release he'd experienced sent him into deep slumber.

The next morning, the jailer brought him two cups of coffee and two hunks of warm bread. It satisfied him for a while but it really hadn't been enough. Later that day, after his lunch, the jailer came for him, a look of dismay on his face.

"Are you okay?" the jailer asked in hushed tones. "Are you bleeding? Did he hurt you?"

"No. He was very kind."

The jailer looked startled but said nothing. When Denny arrived at the office a few minutes later, he had to cover his raging erection with his hands. The sight of his arousal sent Christoph into mad laughter the moment they were alone.

"I think you missed me." Christoph pushed Denny over his desk, whipped down his trousers and sucked his ass.

Nobody had ever touched Denny there, let alone put their mouth, oh Lord, right *there*. He'd never heard of such a thing, but when Christoph buried his face in Denny's ass and licked, Denny came so fast his juices shot all over the desk, before he could stop himself.

Christoph chuckled and cleaned up the mess with one of Denny's grimy socks. He turned Denny around, almost bringing him to another feverish orgasm, but this time, Christoph played with himself and when Denny could take it no longer, Christoph threw everything off the desk and pulled Denny up and over the desk until Denny lay on his back. Christoph climbed over him as his work materials clattered to the floor. Christoph pointed his rigid cock over Denny's mouth. His shaft was surprisingly meaty. Thick and huge. Denny had feared the man might have a puny appendage. He'd glimpsed a few of his shipmates' dicks and had been horrified. What a joy to be here in this office with a man who had such a mighty penis for Denny's gratification.

Christoph showed Denny how to bring a man to ultimate bliss too. He taught him how to suck a cock without teeth grazing the fragile skin. All the while, as Denny brought new delights to the man who was keeping him imprisoned, he daydreamed he was with another, nameless, faceless, man, who sought only an uninterrupted pleasure cruise with Denny.

All the next day, Christoph sent for Denny numerous times. He was an impatient lover, eager to come then send Denny back to his cell.

"Why does your stomach rumble?" he complained late in

the afternoon.

"Because you don't feed me enough. You don't feed any of us what we need to eat to survive."

Christoph looked so surprised that Denny wanted to punch the man in the face.

"I will see to it that you have plenty of food tonight," Christoph assured him, sending Denny away with a wave of his hand.

He was as good as his word. That night, the scent of lemon and garlic wafted down the dark corridor of the jail house. Denny and the others clung to the bars of their cells, anxious for whatever it was that was making such delicious smells. Denny was salivating by the time he received his plate of fish, yellow rice and black beans. He sat against the cold wall of his cell, holding the warm plate in his hands, unable to believe the feast before him. The guard even brought him a glass of red wine.

That night, when Christoph sent for him, his shipmates murmured, "Thank you, Denny," as he moved past them.

"Thank you for your sacrifice," the last man said.

Denny and the guard exchanged looks. Denny felt no shame that he was actually enjoying his little trysts with Christoph. It was nobody's business but his.

In Christoph's office, Denny waited for his instructions but Christoph pointed to a side table where a steaming bowl of water and a large cake of soap awaited him.

"You smell terrible," Christoph complained. "You must bathe. I have also provided you with clean socks."

Denny removed his clothing and washed quickly, enjoying the hot suds against his cold body. Christoph gave him another glass of wine, and Denny grew bolder once he realized Christoph was desperate for their sexual contact.

"If we are to do this, then you must feed me and the others properly tomorrow."

Christoph stared at him. "Were you not fed well tonight?"

"Yes, but tomorrow is another day." He gave Christoph what he hoped was a confident smile. "And the others must be allowed to bathe too."

Christoph frowned. "You think your mouth is so talented, boy?"

It must be, otherwise you wouldn't stare at it so hard. "If it doesn't please you, I can always return to my cell."

"Oh! So dramatic." Christoph frowned. "Get on your knees. Now."

When Denny didn't budge, Christoph said, "All right. Food and bathing." He waved his hand. "For all."

Denny gave Christoph a cock-sucking he suspected his captor would never forget, sliding his fingers into Christoph's tight asshole. Christoph bucked and jerked against Denny's intrusions, chanting, "*Si, si*," over and over again.

Once again, there were no shared moments of tenderness beyond Christoph's carnal release. Denny loved the taste of semen and looked forward to repeating his performance the following day, but wondered why Christoph had stopped touching him.

"Don't play with yourself," Christoph admonished. "I will know if you do. I have something special planned for tomorrow night."

Denny returned to his cell, aware of the other men's scrutiny. "Was it terrible?" one of the men whispered to him.

"No." And the truth was that it wasn't.

For the next two days, Denny and the rest of the crew bathed, ate well, and even received clean clothes. Meanwhile, Denny and Christoph continued to meet, Denny bringing Christoph to intense fulfillment in the jailer's office. Whatever plans he'd had for Denny seemed forgotten. On the third morning, Denny received a cup of coffee and a hunk of bread.

"What about the others?" Denny asked, when he saw his meager offerings.

"Everyone has the same thing." The guard stared down at him a moment then left, a secretive smile on his face.

Denny didn't take this sitting or lying down. He yelled at the others from the bars of his cell, "I'll see this right!"

He didn't have to wait long. By the afternoon, Christoph wanted him again but Denny told the guard, "No. You tell him to feed us properly and allow us to bathe, or I will never come to his office again."

The guard seemed scandalized. "I can't tell him that." He narrowed his eyes. "He'll whip you."

Denny became aware of the others staring at him from their cell bars and he lost his temper. "So what? I've done everything he's asked of me and now he's feeding us mere scraps again." He sat against the wall, arms folded.

The guard left, looking disgruntled. Denny wondered what would happen to him and pictured himself, Christ-like, being flogged within an inch of his life. He didn't care much in that moment. Life was horrible. He folded his arms around his body and tried to imagine he was warm. His head, back, and every other part of his body, ached with hunger and sleeping on the cold stone floor night after night.

He was astonished when thirty minutes later, the guards scurried along the cells, unlocking each one and handing out bowls of porridge, pieces of fruit, more coffee and bread, and apologies.

Except for Denny.

"He wants to see you," the guard said, looking petrified.

Denny followed him along the corridor. None of Denny's shipmates looked up or said a word. They were too busy eating. The guard knocked on Christoph's door and opened it without waiting for a response. He pushed Denny inside the office with a vicious shove then closed the door behind him.

Christoph spoke half an inch from Denny's face. "I ought to kill you. I can't stop thinking of you. You've made a mockery of my marriage. I can't bear for her to touch me. I have to get drunk in order to pleasure her. I hate it when she touches me. Why couldn't you be a woman?"

56

Denny almost laughed, except that he realized Christoph was in true anguish. Christoph kissed him with the kind of hunger born of carnal need. Their kisses grew heated and long, until Christoph pulled away.

"This may be our last time, so honor my desire. Fuck me. And fuck me hard. Though I want you to handcuff me, as though I am your prisoner. Cuff my hands and take me from behind."

Denny felt such a flame of desire it seemed to burn him from within. He couldn't speak. He grabbed Christoph and kissed him, as Christoph rubbed against him. The searing heat between their crushed bodies was almost more than Denny could handle.

Christoph dropped to his knees, fumbled with the buttons on Denny's prison-issue pants and released his now rigid cock, letting his tongue capture it. He licked and sucked frantically, reaching to encircle and hold Denny's balls. Christoph came off Denny's cock and rasped, "Fuck me!" He stood, his own erection straining inside his trousers. Christoph reached into a desk drawer and extracted a pair of hand irons, or, as Denny knew them to be known, handcuffs. They were an old, solid pair that looked a little rusty but Christoph seemed so excited it ignited Denny's own wicked desires. He leaned Christoph over his desk, whipped down his trousers and licked the man's ass.

Christoph moaned, his strong, muscular thighs rippling as Denny tried to spread Christoph's legs. Christoph kicked off his shoes, wearing only his long black socks, and spread his legs, allowing Denny closer access to his hole. Denny licked him some more. Christoph gripped the desk and panted. "I don't want to come like this. I want you to bind me and fuck me hard."

Denny took his tongue out of Christoph's ass. "Believe me, I will." He was so turned on he couldn't think straight.

This was all so new for Denny, but he easily took command of the man bent before him. He resumed licking and Christoph uttered a guttural cry as he came all over his nice, shiny desk. Denny swept up the juices with his fingers and smeared Christoph's ass with the hot liquid. Christoph jumped when Denny slapped his ass again, then pulled his arms behind his back.

"You sure this is what you want?" Denny asked, aware that this was a pivotal point from which he could never return.

"Yes, yes. I beg of you." Christoph put his head to the table.

Denny cuffed his jailer's hands and pointed his cock at Christoph's hole.

"Fuck me hard!" Christoph begged.

Denny felt an astonishing fire soaring within him as he slid his cock inside Christoph's tight, hot space. Nothing compared with being inside a man. Not a man's mouth or hand, or even Denny's own hand. He could feel everything going on inside Christoph's body, the quivering pleasure he received from Denny's incessant pounding. Denny came at the same moment Christoph let out a loud groan.

"Oh, joy. Don't stop. Don't stop. Oh. I'm coming! Denny, I am coming!"

Chapter Five

Merritt's abilities sharpened in that cave as he held each bewitched object in his hands. He soon knew who owned what, including a small gold ring that belonged to Denny. Merritt would wear it until he saw Denny again. He slumped against the cave wall, remembering that his sister had said Denny would soon be here. She could only know that if he'd been arrested and would face trial for his crimes.

The trials on the island were often harrowing.

His sister was on probation with the court, forbidden from bewitching another soul. Instead of following the judge's orders, she'd hexed her own cousin. How long had she been doing this to Gremma? Merritt would put a stop to it. He would find a way to stop all of it.

A heavy rain fell from the sky and he huddled against the chill. He was hungrier than ever now. Oh, the sandwich! It hadn't been poisoned so he could eat it. He glanced at his hands. His previously cursed, blackened fingertips were their normal color once more. He had to wash them, though, after all that negative magic had moved through them.

He had a plan but a clear mind would help him execute it.

Why had Cillian died if the apple hadn't been poisoned? What had killed him? He'd seen his sister cutting his shoulder, but Cillian had had no wound when Merritt had found him in the stables. Wait. Avery was from the elf community and their magic cured animals' wounds. Merritt would ask him, but suspected that Avery must have found the cut and assumed that Cillian had injured himself on a tree branch and had healed him.

Merritt stepped outside and let the rain wash over him. He'd danced in the rain on the deck of the La-Di-Da with Denny. They'd laughed and sung songs, until Fortunata had appeared, furious, and the dancing had stopped.

Soaked now, he moved back into the cave, feeling refreshed. Thankful for his hiding place, he dropped to the floor and opened the package containing the sandwich. He ate fast. Perfect. He slumped against the wall again, trying to ignore the rumbles of hunger still scratching at him from within.

Just a little bit of rest and he'd set out at dawn and confront Gremma. He'd restore her natural beauty and force her to no longer hex people. He knew how he would do it, too. He'd threaten her with an unbreakable hex she could never lift. That nobody could lift.

He'd turn her into a Scylla, a six-headed, twelve-footed sea monster, destined to spend her days alone in the ocean hunting for food and being hunted by those who desired to kill such beasts. Merritt grinned at his own creativity. It was an especially cunning idea, considering Gremma was deathly afraid of the sea.

Merritt tried to settle into sleep, dozing on and off. Denny's face was there, smiling and laughing. "My love." Merritt reached out to him from his dreams.

* * * *

Denny awakened from his sleep late in the afternoon when Barthelmass returned with a jug of mulled cider. His dream of Christoph seemed so real he looked across the room expecting to see his former shipmates' cells from the bars of his own, but they weren't there. A strange emotion tugged at him. Merritt had hovered over the edge of the dream and it devastated him. *Why do I feel as though I cheated on him when I didn't even know him then?*

Without him, Denny felt as though life was imprisonment. Denny's father, who'd had little education, was fond of

60

quoting some old French philosopher who'd apparently said, 'Man is free but is everywhere in chains.' True enough. The heat from the fireplace in Christoph's office no longer warmed him. Back to reality, he remembered returning to his cold cell. This was a different cell in another time and place. He wasn't free. He was everywhere in chains.

Barthelmass' voice invaded his thoughts. "It's non-alcoholic, so drink up." He'd also brought a hearty bowl of fish stew and a thick hunk of fresh, hot, crusty bed.

Denny sat at the little table and ate with gusto. He wondered if Ebba had made this. She'd certainly prepared him many a good meal during her time with him until she had left the ship. He was certain she'd been asked to be set free in Tenerife. He was convinced things had been good between them. How had he not known of her curse?

He nibbled at his bread. *Maybe she asked me before we were both cursed and I forgot about it. She got off my ship, though. In one piece.* He suddenly remembered her reference to having two husbands. He couldn't help asking Barthelmass, who chuckled. "Yes, she was married twice. Dead unlucky she was. Both drowned at sea. Left her quite rich."

Denny listened, wondering if she'd offed her husbands for their wealth. As though Barthelmass could read his thoughts he said, "Doesn't matter how rich a woman is, if she is cursed, no amount of money can shift it."

"And the prince won't allow you to marry?"

"Some people are destined for sadness." Barthelmass sighed, looking so unhappy Denny felt miserable for the poor fellow.

Denny stared at him. What a strange thing for Barthelmass to say. It was not the first time Denny had heard these words. A twinge of angst hit him between the eyes and made his wings twitch.

"Excellent!" Barthelmass seemed pleased, forgetting his own concerns as he touched Denny's feathers.

Denny was lost in thought, still shaky from his dream. He'd never seen Christoph again after Piggins had procured the crew's release. Christoph had stayed in his office when Denny and the others had left their cells. Whatever had occurred between him and Denny remained their secret. The other crewmembers had treated Denny kindly after that, believing Denny had given of himself to save all their asses. It was partly true, but he'd enjoyed his time with Christoph. His incarceration had allowed him to explore his own sexuality and he found he wanted, and deeply desired, men.

Denny never said so, but other men who were so inclined drifted toward him once he took over the ship and renamed her. Freedom came with piracy, and he had a lot more success than some. He had often dreamed of returning to the port in Tarragona, and had done one time, about three years after his imprisonment. Christoph had no longer worked at the jail but when he'd asked a few locals in one of the tavernas, the innkeeper had remembered him.

"He was a sad one. They say he was married but was in love with another." He dropped his voice. "They say it was a man. One of his prisoners. He left the island long ago. Hasn't been seen since."

Denny might never know if he himself had been the prisoner Christoph had loved, but when he was honest with himself he realized he probably wasn't. They'd shared an intense physical connection but their contact had been brief. Denny had learned over the years that sensuality did not mean love. Men could share the highest form of intimacy and not have genuine love feelings for one another. Denny had found lovers who pleased him, and he them, but until he'd met Merritt, love had eluded him.

Barthelmass urged Denny to work his wings again, but this time wouldn't touch Denny to help him. Denny tried hard and managed to get some action, and he did until his still-sore wing smacked the wall and sent spirals of pain shooting through his back and shoulder.

"You're getting there. Wait until you can fly. You won't regret your curse then."

"How do you know? You don't have wings, do you?"

"Well," Barthelmass demurred, "my ladylove says my cock flies her to the moon."

Denny winced. "I could have lived without knowing that."

Barthelmass shrugged. "You asked."

True enough. Denny finished every last bite of food and drink then finally plucked up enough courage to look at his face in the mirror above his desk. He looked horrible.

"We'll send somebody to give you a shave later," Barthelmass promised. "And we need to take care of your straggly hair."

Straggly? Denny touched his sparse hair that had once been long and luxurious. He looked an old man. An old man with wings. *Cripes. I'm never gonna get laid again.* What the hell had happened to him?

"You haven't been sipping nectar," Barthelmass told him. "You're a fairy. You're supposed to drink flower nectar and honey. Don't worry. We can make you look okay. You know what? Frogmorten can help you."

"Who?"

"The humanized bumblebee. He pollinates flowers all the time. If you ask him nicely, I bet he can accommodate you."

"Can you ask him to come and see me?"

"Sure thing." He glanced at Denny. "He'll expect repayment."

"I'm sure he will." Denny didn't mind. Thanks to Barthelmass' interference with his person, Denny was gagging for some cock. But the bee man didn't turn up for a couple of hours, during which time Denny fell into the trap of letting memories from his past come back to haunt him.

He plunged back to the time he, his father and Polly had been forced to enter a spike, or workhouse, because his father was behind on his payments for basic things like rent. Denny's mum was gone. But that was another story.

Denny was ten years old and the New Poor Law had been passed. Adults as well as children could be admitted and forced to

63

work as a way to pay off debts. Denny, and Polly, who was eight, spent the eleven months the family was confined in the workhouse picking oakum, which would later be used to fill the hulls and working joints of ships.

"You are helping your country," their overseer would say, his voice booming as he paced between rows of virtual slaves bent to their tasks.

Denny hated the work, which involved picking apart old cords and rope with a metal spike – hence the nickname for the workhouse – and rolling the coarse threads into balls. Polly cried a lot but managed to get some work done. Their father had the worst job. He had to crush human bones to use for fertilizer. Though the work was easy, the new law meant lots of people kept coming to the workhouse and food was scarce. His father admitted to Denny one night that some of the starving men fought over the bones so they could suck out the marrow before crushing them.

Denny wasn't as disgusted as he should have been. He wouldn't have minded a bit of bone marrow. He didn't mind the food and, being the children of neglectful parents, he and Polly were fed better in the spike than they had been at home. They got bread and porridge for breakfast. Though porridge was a staple British breakfast item, it had never been something Denny and Polly had eaten before, and it became his lifelong obsession. Polly preferred dinner, and he liked it too, especially when they got the rare treats of cheese, butter and potatoes with their bread and pickled meats.

Their father, however, was never the same after their time in the workhouse and soon vanished once they were released. What had once been their home, a basement flat in East London, was now overrun by numerous displaced families. Denny, at the ripe old age of eleven, wound up on the streets finding ways to make money to pay for Polly's keep in the apartment. She worked occasionally as a chimney sweep with Denny some days, hiding her long locks under a cap so she could pass for a boy. Denny tried to look out for her, but was soon working in a cotton factory where he spent long days waterproofing the fiber with rubber gum, which was then used to produce Mackintosh coats.

Polly was too young by law to work in factories because she was *not yet nine. She had learned to steal and managed to snatch a loaf of bread or a potato here and there, but Denny's long hours in the factory kept him away from her. By the time he went to the apartment to find her one Christmas Eve, he learned that the people he'd been giving money to, to care for her, had sold her off as a junior housemaid. He tried so hard to find her but learned right after New Year that she had been arrested for stealing a loaf of bread.*

Now eleven, she was legally old enough to work, but it took Denny almost a whole other year to discover that she had been taken in by a British officer and his wife. Denny traveled to their home in Somerset, only to learn that they'd set sail for Botany Bay in Sydney, Australia. The officer had just been appointed in a position of authority at the penal colony. Denny became frantic. His mother had been banished there for stealing an onion. He'd learned of her circumstances and feared Polly winding up the same way. He decided there and then at the age of thirteen that he would become a seaman and make his way to Australia to rescue his sister, if not his mother.

It would take another four years for Denny to make good on his promise to himself.

"Wake up," a gravelly voice snapped him out of his reverie as somebody viciously shook him, making Denny's tender wing throb with pain.

"What is it?" Denny almost fell off the bed. "What's wrong?" He looked up to see Frogmorten, the bumblebee man, standing over Denny, a large pewter mug in his hand.

"Barthelmass said to bring this to you. He said you needed it."

"Is that nectar?"

Frogmorten nodded. When Denny reached for it, he snatched it back. "How am I to be paid for this elixir of life?"

Denny worked hard not to act on the kind of violent thoughts that had gotten him into so much trouble in the past.

"If you let me have the nectar now, I can show you how I

65

intend to repay you."

"I—" Frogmorten blinked as Denny held his gaze. They exchanged the kind of silent contract only men can sign between them. He gulped. "Okay." He let Denny take the goblet.

Denny drank every drop, ecstatic at the taste of the nectar. Oh, it was the most delicious thing that had ever touched his tongue. *Wait a minute.* The perpetual ache from his wings went away. His muddled thoughts vanished. Nothing hurt. He felt fantastic.

"Can you get me more?" he asked, excited that he could move his wings with total ease. Denny was learning how to stretch his wings, literally, without hitting the wall. *I can't wait to see if I can fly.*

"I'll get you more. You pay me first."

Denny didn't hesitate. He sat on the bed and undid Frogmorten's cotton pants. The bumblebee man's cock was half hard and very generously proportioned. His entire body from the neck down was human and he was quite sexy underneath his clothing. The sight of that huge shaft made Denny drool. He was surprised at the sweetness of the gigantic cock in his grip. Did all of the men here come so well endowed? Now that Denny thought of it, bees consumed only nectar and pollen. He longed to drink a long, cool glass of nectar. It was his new drug of choice. This was what he thought about as he brought Frogmorten carnal pleasure. Denny enjoyed giving a man the ultimate satisfaction with his mouth. Frogmorten's ropey juices flowed quickly down Denny's throat. He moaned, and his cock wouldn't go down.

"You want it again?" Denny asked.

Before Frogmorten could respond, Denny dipped his head and began the whole process of sucking and licking the huge cock again. Frogmorten had made no sound during the first time around, except for the occasional, delirious sigh. This time, he groaned...the sound so unusual yet so erotic to the seasoned pirate that Denny was soon on his knees, moving his hand to Frogmorten's balls and squeezing them. Frogmorten twitched at this unexpected contact, but did not otherwise resist. In fact, he seemed to thrust even harder into Denny's open mouth.

Frogmorten came hard and reached out one massive hand to hold Denny's head to him. When at last Frogmorten stopped coming, Denny knelt back on his haunches.

"I think you enjoy paying your debts," Frogmorten murmured.

"Very much." Denny looked him right in the eye. He was aware of a rush of heat to his own cock and wished he could jerk off quickly, but Frogmorten had other things on his mind.

"I will bring you more nectar. And you will give me more...joy." He left the cell, taking the empty goblet with him. When Frogmorten returned later, he was about to receive payment for the second goblet when Ebba and Barthelmass arrived.

"They've stepped up your trial." Ebba looked upset.

Barthelmass was carrying another basin of water and set it on the table. "The prince has a keen interest in this case and he only leaves the castle at night. He won't come to court in the morning."

Ebba grimaced at Denny. "And I am sorry to tell you that my brother is one of the crown's witnesses against you."

Denny shrugged. His wing felt wonderful.

"It's twitching!" Ebba gasped. "You got it to work!"

"I did. With Barthelmass' help."

"Good, good." Ebba pointed to the goblet. "Drink that nectar. Each cup lasts about two hours. We may have time to get you another cup before your trial starts."

Barthelmass stepped forward and said, "I'll shave him while you coach him."

"Okay."

"But first, Denny's going to wash his teeth. His breath smells like he ate a dead person."

Denny said nothing. He swallowed his nectar then

grabbed the toothbrush and the canister of dental powder Barthelmass handed him and brushed. After using the bowl of water that Barthelmass had brought to swig and gargle, he spat the contents into his empty nectar cup. His mouth felt a lot better afterward and he tried to remember the last time he'd practiced good oral hygiene.

"The more flower nectar you drink, the better your teeth will get. When you manifest your full powers you'll never need to brush them again," Ebba said. She stood at Denny's side as Barthelmass lathered up Denny's head and face. He shaved Denny with a double-edged razor. That was a delight he had previously only ever experienced on the rare times he had visited a barber. His skin stung until Barthelmass dabbed his hands with some kind of tonic from a brown bottle and pressed his palms to Denny's cheeks. The tonic smelled unusual but felt very good.

"What is that?" Denny took a deep sniff.

"Witch hazel. Very good for the skin." Barthelmass turned Denny's chair around and leaned him back, washing his hair and scalp with the cold water and a bar of white soap. He tilted Denny's head up again and dried his head with a rough cloth.

Ebba kept grilling Denny, who could hardly concentrate on what she was saying.

"Don't forget to mention your mother leaving you. Oh, and your dad deserting you. There are four women on the jury and they will feel sympathy for you."

"Okay."

"And mention your sister. Don't forget to talk about the workhouse and your years working as a child slave in the factory. Keep your stories of thieving to a minimum. Oh. I will talk about your freeing the slaves. By the time I'm done with you, the women on the jury will be weeping to save you."

"And the best I can look forward to is life in prison?"

"Maybe not that long. You might get time off for good behavior. But I can almost guarantee I won't let you be executed."

"Thanks." Denny was worried now. She could *almost* guarantee it?

Barthelmass clipped at Denny's hair with an expert touch. Denny was drowsy from the sensation of having another man touch him again. And anyone touching his head brought a sense of physical comfort. If he could spend the rest of his life in this cell experiencing moments like this he could die happy.

When he was done, Barthelmass stood back and said, "I think I've missed my true calling. You're very dashing now, Pirate Denny." He hoisted the mirror from the wall and put it into Denny's hands.

Denny was thrilled with the way he looked. His hair was cut close to his scalp and wasn't so unkempt-looking anymore. He had remnants of a three-day growth on his chin and upper lip but no longer looked like a pitiful old man straight out of a Charles Dickens story.

He bantered back and forth with Ebba, whose intense questioning gave Denny an unpleasant taste of what he should expect in the courtroom.

"Is there anything I should know about you? Some big secret that could get you the death sentence and me looking like a buffoon?" Ebba asked, as Denny dressed in the smart-looking clothes she and Barthelmass had brought him.

His entire ensemble was black. Black pants and shirt and soft, moccasin-type shoes in black. They were the most comfortable things Denny had ever worn. If one was to receive a death sentence, at least the locals wanted you to go out with ease. He thought of other pirates he knew who'd faced horrible trials with stocks and gallows. If he were to die this day at least he didn't wobble in his broken heel. He missed his boots, though. They made him feel sexy and stylish. The moccasins just made him want to curl up and sleep.

"I have many secrets. But there's one I guess I should tell you. My name isn't really Denny."

She frowned. "What is it then?"

Denny hesitated. It was true that Denny had secrets. Plenty of them. The worst was that his first name was really Dunstan Derrick. "My name is Dunstan," he said.

Ebba and Barthelmass exchanged uncomprehending looks.

"With the British habit of condensing every single name in the book, I became Dunny. And dunnies are toilets. I could not live with their ridicule had they known my real name. Therefore, I could *not* keep sharing a name with a bloody lavatory. So I became Denny." Aye, he had secrets. And he had plans. If he could wheedle himself a prison conviction he could cope with that. It would give him hope that he would see his prince again. Not that he could mention *that* in court. But also, while he waited, he wouldn't mind indulging in his wild fantasies of being handed around by a bunch of horny men to use. He *craved* men. Not that he could mention that in court either.

One way or another, he would escape and find his freedom again. He could change his name. Reinvent himself. He'd done it before and he could do it again.

"We'll mention it under the guise of your coming clean and being honest," Ebba said.

"I *am* coming clean and being honest."

"No other secrets?"

"I have some, but nothing I wish to declare," Denny said.

The cell door rattled and the green-winged man entered. "Ah," he said. "You look much better. How's our wing project progressing?"

"We've got it sorted." Denny showed the green-winged man that he could make his wings open up and flap, and he even rose a little from the ground.

"Have you mastered flying yet?"

"I've been locked in this cell. Not much room to fly."

"Oh, yeah. Of course. Right." He scribbled something in his book, and Denny had a hunch it wasn't flattering.

"Are we ready?" the green-winged man asked.

"We are." Ebba sounded a lot more confident than Denny felt.

Being executed had never been on his to-do list. Ever. He knew one day he would die but he'd become excited when he'd learned that being a fairy had given him immortal powers. He had to explore them and enjoy them, didn't he?

They all left the cell and walked down the corridor. Denny realized everyone in his little party was wearing black and white clothing. He soon became distracted by a heavenly scent on the air. A spicy stew of some sort. *I hope they give me a last supper if I'm condemned to die. And maybe one last shag.* Food and sex. His favorite things in the world. Denny and the others passed from the jail to a bridge that hovered over a moat. He thought he saw a dead man's body floating beneath him but didn't look too hard. The bridge was flimsy and made of rope and wood. He grasped the rope handles, remembering his hard work picking oakum. He'd been a marked man since day one.

The others also clutched the bridge's handles.

"Everyone all right?" Ebba asked.

"Yes, thanks," the others reported back to her with varying degrees of enthusiasm.

Denny was scared now. This wasn't too far from walking the plank. For the first time in his adult life, he knew mind-numbing, stark-staring fear. It didn't taste too good. He said nothing, though, and followed the others into another section of the building. Lit sconces held by invisible hands lined the corridor. Denny couldn't see the people holding them but heard their whispery voices.

"Let me see them," Denny murmured to his fairy wings. The wings twitched and vibrated, and Denny gasped, holding his breath as the beings materialized. They all looked like black fairies with spider webs for wings and red eyes.

"He can see us," one of them said to the others. All eyes trained on him, and Denny gave them a wave. They were quite beautiful actually, even though they projected a

71

naughtiness he hadn't expected from fairies. They smacked and spat at each other and at others walking past them.

"That's the Unseelie Court," Ebba said, turning around to Denny. She came back and walked beside him. "I'm glad you can see them. It bolsters your case."

"How so?"

"You're tapping into your magic and leaving your human side behind you."

"And that's a good thing?"

"Of course it is. The Unseelie Court members are the naughty ones. Those that are here are doing community service for small crimes."

"What's a small crime?"

"Frightening cattle, starting thunderstorms, hiding old ladies' wigs, putting boils on people's bottoms, having sex with humans. Oh, here we are." She stopped speaking and led Denny into the most gorgeous room he had ever seen. The place was teeming with winged creatures of every kind imaginable. A winged horse stood at the front of the court on the left side. A centaur stood on the right.

"We're case number three," Ebba told Denny as a see-through pink fairy flew over to her and tossed Ebba a black and white envelope marked with the number three.

Ebba and Barthelmass flanked Denny as they took their seats. For the first time, Denny wasn't troubled by his wings. They seemed to know what to do and hugged his back like soft pillows.

"Nice," Ebba said to him. "Your wings are working with you. The only ones allowed to fly in the court house are the Seelie fairies, the goody-two shoes who work for the judge."

"What's he like?" Denny asked.

"He doesn't say much but when he does, he's brutal." Ebba pored over the contents of the envelope and lapsed into silence. Denny had never sat in anything as comfortable as the chair in which he reclined. He was afraid he'd fall asleep so he focused instead on the long, black and white bench at the front of the room. It looked like it was made of marble. Its harlequin pattern mirrored the designs on the wall. This motif continued across the ceiling with black and white glass showing images of fairy wings, treetops and the occasional bird breaking into song. The court seats were luxurious, plush white velvet. Many people had removed their shoes. There was much scrunching of toes in the thick black carpeting. Denny wished he could do it too, but decided that since he was on trial defending his life, he should act with a little decorum.

The chattering and the swoop of birdsong ended as a judge in black robes entered the courtroom and sat in the middle of the long table up front.

"Pegasus, please alert the jury that we're ready," he said, sounding feeble and weak.

"Who said that?" the judge shouted, his gaze sweeping the courtroom.

Everyone froze.

"Who said I'm old and past it?"

A quiet panic seemed to descend on all those present.

Pegasus, the winged horse, whinnied and stamped his foot. Doors on either side of the room opened, and four men and four women entered, taking their seats beside the judge. Finally a blue-winged male fairy raised his hand.

"It was I, Your Honor. I humbly apologize."

"Well, since you spoke up, I'll forgive you. Next time you lose a wing."

The man's face turned red. "Yes, your honor. Thank you, your honor." He took a seat, his face bright red.

Denny watched him and saw the poor man's hand was shaking as he ran it over his face. *Oh, boy, this judge is gonna be a barrel of laughs.* Denny slumped in his seat, wondering how quickly into his trial the judge would have Denny killed.

"First case," the judge bawled. "Come on. I want to go home. I'm missing the dragon-slaying semi-finals for this!"

The courtroom broke into an ethereal titter. The judge

73

banged his gavel. "Where's the defendant?"

Every head turned as a man rose and walked down the stairs. He wore similar prison-issue clothes to Denny, who recognized the guy with the eagle head and one wing.

"What's with everything being black and white?" Denny whispered to Ebba.

"The judge sees the world that way. Everything is black and white."

That wasn't a good thing when Denny knew there were many shades between the two. This judge was going to be tough and probably merciless.

The man picking his way across the crowded courtroom seemed frail and shaky and finally reached the witness box, a wooden affair that rose from the ground. Once the man stepped inside, the box sprouted wrought-iron bars and hovered high above the courtroom participants.

Denny was petrified, but also fascinated. He glanced at the jury members but realized he could get a better look at them once he took the witness stand. He tried not to fret as he took in the fortress-like cage.

"Why are you here?" the judge asked the eagle man.

"Because I was arrested, your honor."

"I know that, funny man."

The crowd tittered but the judge spoke over the ripple of laughter, "What are your charges?"

"Ah. Piracy." The eagle man looked pleased with himself.

The judge folded his hands and leaned on the bench, studying the accused. "Do you dispute the charges?"

"I don't know. I haven't heard them yet."

The judge glanced up and down the row of jurors, who kept leaning into one another, whispering. Denny had never seen women on a jury before, but he'd also never seen jurors gossiping and giggling during a trial either.

"You are charged with capital crimes. You are a menace to the high seas. Do you deny it?" the judge asked.

The eagle man said, "Your honor, there is a French proverb that states, 'One meets his destiny often in the road

74

he takes to avoid it.'"

"And what the hell is that supposed to mean?"

"I tried to make an honest living, but being a pirate is a lot more fun."

The courtroom erupted with appreciative laughter. Denny hid a smirk, frightened that any display of support of a man on trial might harm his own case. He stared at the eagle man who continued to banter with the judge. It was only when the eagle man said, "Your honor, I was cursed by the princess of this island," that Denny saw the anger behind the careless quips.

He didn't know how it was possible, but Denny recognized him in that moment as the Pirate Howard deGacy. He had been caught and tried and was supposed to hang in the United States several years ago. Somehow he'd escaped but his longtime pirating buddy 'Don' Pedro Gilbert, with whom he'd pillaged and plundered up and down the Florida Straits had been hanged for piracy in Boston, Massachusetts six years ago.

"For the record, what is your name?" the judge asked him.

"Percy Humbridge, your honor."

Howard deGacy was famous for offering up phony names, and this time was no exception.

Denny leaned in to Ebba and said, "He's lying. I know his real name. If I offer it up to the court, will it help my own case?"

"We could try," she said. She got to her feet, raising a hand. "Your honor, if it pleases the court, my client has information about this prisoner. He can testify to the fact that this man is lying about his name."

"Who says so?" Howard deGacy shot to his feet and stared down at Denny with pure hatred in his eyes. "You," he snarled. "I should have killed you when I had the chance."

"That's what they all say," Denny responded, giving deGacy his best, most disarming smile.

75

Chapter Six

The rain stopped at dawn and the sudden break in its relentless rhythm awakened Merritt, who roused himself from sleep. He peered outside. The faint light of day beckoned him. He picked up every object before him, careful to wrap the black candle in the packaging from his sandwich. Merritt put everything in his pockets, except his wax-filled shoes. The strange magic Gremma and Fortunata had cast to keep Merritt locked in a perpetual cycle of sleep and despair angered him. He picked up the shoes and, outside the cave, took a deep breath.

He loved the natural world and the land hummed to him. He was regaining his senses bit by bit. He walked down the mountain and found a spot under a yew tree. He used one of the shoes to dig a hole and whispered a few words of an old incantation and the sodden earth dried up long enough for him to dig without the mud sloshing back in again.

Things are coming back to me. Things I thought I'd forgotten. Things I didn't realize had been stolen from me.

He dug faster now, eager to break the spell. Yew had protective qualities, and two feet down, he buried one of the shoes. Farther down the slope, he found another yew and buried the second one.

Leaning on his haunches for a moment, he realized he didn't feel different, even though he'd broken the curse. Actually, he did feel different. He wasn't perpetually sleepy. Even with little sleep in the cave he felt alive, vibrant. It was a wonderful feeling. Covered in mud now, he kept moving down the mountain, more cheerful than he'd been in months.

Wait. Has it been months? How long ago did we leave Denny's ship? Sometimes it feels like forever, other times it feels recent. He knew he'd have to start reading his sister's mind to figure out what was really going on. He was in such a good mood, he'd walked a mile before he realized it. And he reached the blacksmith's forge. He was surprised to see it shuttered. Even in such awful weather there was always the need for Smitty's exquisite workmanship. He turned out everything from tools and weapons to horseshoes and cooking pots. The need for these things never stopped.

Even his house seemed empty.

"What do you want?" a raspy voice came from behind when Merritt peered through the front windows. He turned, but couldn't see Smitty at first.

"Down 'ere," the raspy voice went on, and Merritt looked down to find the blacksmith leaning against a tree trunk, a cup of tea in his hand. "You don't want to know how long it took me to make this." Smitty glowered as he held up his cup. "I can't even make fire anymore! I had to bribe one of my wee kiddies into making a fire, and they're not supposed to do that." He slurped at his tea. "Fine cup of tea, though. Can I interest you in one?"

Merritt hesitated. He sensed every awful thing that had happened to the poor man and wanted to put him out of his misery and move on to Fortunata's next unfortunate victim, but on the other hand, he wanted an ally in Smitty. And he longed for something warm.

"I would enjoy that, thank you."

"It's a chipped cup, and I'm sorry about that, but we've few to spare. I've had to sell off everything just to survive. I have no tools left, and my striker—do you know young Walter?" Before Merritt could respond, Smitty barreled on, "Well, he developed a strange case of warts all over his body and boils on his bottom."

Oh no. That sounds like Fortunata's handiwork.

"And he was no longer able to help me produce tools." Smitty looked devastated. "It caused him untold agony to lift the sledgehammer. He had to quit, and I sold the sledgehammer, too." He poured Merritt his tea then handed him the cup.

"What happened to you?" Merritt asked.

"That witch. Gremma. She put a spell on me. That's what she did. She turned me into a bleedin' fairy, then that Gremma laughed. Everyone knows fairies are allergic to iron. Why did she do that to me?" Poor Smitty looked confused.

"You've been cursed," Merritt said.

"I know that. I've got wings. Wings, for Lord's sake. Whoever heard of a gnome with wings? Do you see them?" His voice rose, and Merritt nodded.

"Aye, I see your wings." They were big and black and hairy, and sort of matched the thick thatch of hair atop Smitty's head. He was tall for a gnome, but then he was part human and ogre as well. What had he done to displease Fortunata? Merritt tried to read Smitty's mind but Smitty was too busy thinking angry thoughts about Gremma.

"I knew Gremma had been banished from the palace, for what reasons I was never clear, but she's lived happily among us all here in the forest. Never had a cross word with her. Suddenly she's stomping around my house uninvited and muttering something weird. And have you seen her face lately?" He winced.

Merritt saw it all unspooling in his mind. *Oh, boy.* Time was of the essence.

"She cursed you by stealing this." Merritt reached into his pocket and extracted the small iron dagger he'd found on Gremma's altar. "I've removed the hex on it, but you are going to have to bury this someplace far and deep from here."

"Why'd she do it to me?" Tears formed in his eyes. It wasn't a pretty sight.

"She did it at someone else's bidding."

"Of course! I should have realized. People tell me she cries all night. She's cursed lots of us, you know."

"Yes. Now look. The magic is broken and your wings, well, I can take care of those, but you must bury the dagger as soon as I've done it." Merritt laid it at Smitty's feet. "In order for me to break the curse completely, I must know what you did to displease Princess Fortunata."

"Fortunata? Why, I did nothing." Smitty's cheeks flamed. "Oh. My missus. My wife was making her a cloak, and the princess said she wasn't working fast enough. She tried to tell the princess we had a young son who was sick. He'd gotten worse and worse. But the princess wouldn't listen and screamed and yelled. She took off and we haven't seen her since. She never picked up the cloak, you know."

"You slept with her," Merritt said, shocked and saddened when he saw the image in his mind.

Smitty gasped. "But that was years ago!"

Merritt got a flash image in his mind of Smitty naked. Merritt gulped. The blacksmith had a massive cock. No wonder his sister had been, er, smitten with Smitty.

"I wasn't married then!" Smitty bawled.

"But she's tried to come back to you."

"Until this happened, relentlessly."

"I'm going to give you a token. You must keep it on you for protection." Merritt reached behind Smitty's back, grabbed a wing and pulled.

Smitty's howl of pain filled the air.

"And bury these, too."

"My wings!" Smitty stared at them. There was only a tiny bit of blood, but Smitty was free of them.

Suddenly, the blacksmith's wife came running out of the house. "Smitty! Smitty! Baby Smythe's stopped coughing!"

Smitty jumped to his feet. "The prince has lifted our curse!"

"Wait now," Merritt said. "Before you get too excited, I need the cloak you were making for my sister."

"It's gone," Smitty's wife said. "Gremma came and took it."

"When?"

"Weeks ago."

Merritt sighed. "I'll go and find it. Now, Smitty, you do as I say. Visit your son, but you must bury that dagger quickly. I have other people to visit. Speak of this to no one. Hurry now."

"How can I thank you?" Smitty asked, spreading his hands.

"You don't owe me thanks. I owe you an apology on my family's behalf. I can assure you both that nothing like this will ever happen again."

"Thank you," Smitty said, and shook his hand.

Merritt pressed the token into Smitty's palm. "Keep this. And should Gremma or Fortunata visit, say only, 'I am under the prince's protection.' Never, ever speak of this token or keep it someplace visible. Good day to you now. I'll come and visit baby Smythe very soon." He didn't wait any longer. Merritt knew exactly what his sister had done and he was furious with her. She wanted control over the whole kingdom and he knew the cloak carried fragments of the possessions of all those whom she'd cursed and whom she planned to attack in the future.

He hurried to Gremma's house, wondering if she was already aware that her evil handiwork was being obliterated.

* * * *

Back in the courtroom, the crowd erupted in wild laughter. Even a couple of jurors joined in until the judge silenced them with a look.

"You!" The judge pointed across the room at Denny. "Tell me what you know of this man."

"Stand up!" Ebba snapped in a low tone.

Denny complied, surprised at how badly his knees were knocking. Any second now, the judge would say, 'Who's there?'

"Come up here and stand beside Pegasus and tell me

what you know," the judge insisted.

Denny hated the idea, but if it bought him a lighter sentence he'd go for it. He made his way down the stairs and soon saw why it had taken deGacy a little time to make his way down the front. Fairies sitting on the stairs kept touching him and grabbing his feet.

At last he made it to the marble desk and stood beside the big, winged horse, who snorted down at him. Denny thought the magnificent creature was lovely. He had always adored horses but a life at sea had given him no access to them. He touched the horse's flank, admiring his physical beauty. The horse's nostrils flared, and Denny removed his hand again.

"Speak!" the judge ordered. Before Denny could start, he added, "And do you still think I sound feeble and weak?"

How embarrassing. "No, your honor."

"Good. Step to it then. Look lively, man."

Denny had to be careful of his thoughts around this courtroom. All eyes were on him as he said, "Pirate deGacy worked in tandem with 'Don' Pedro Gilbert. Together they ran an unusual piracy ring on dry land. They would lure ships from sea into small coves and harbors with fires they set. The ships would arrive and Gilbert and deGacy would attack the ships, taking everything they could and destroying the vessels to hide their deeds."

A murmur went up in the room.

"Somehow, one of the crew members from the last ship they attempted to destroy squeezed through a hatch and freed the rest of the crew. They are the only known survivors of a joint deGacy and Gilbert attack. The two pirates were captured returning to the bay to check on the ship's destruction. They were in prison for almost two years as the United States government worked to learn their true identities. They were tried and sentenced to death. Gilbert was hanged in 1845, but deGacy escaped and here he is today, your honor."

"It's not me," deGacy whined from the witness box. "He's

81

got it all wrong."

"I don't think so," the judge said, his tone soft. "However, this means we have to extradite you back to the United States of America, since they have already sentenced you. Bloody Americans. Such a pain in the ass to deal with."

The judge leaned into the jurors to his right. Denny finally got a closer look at them. There were two women in white, who looked like twins. They were tall and thin and seemed to speak at the same time. A man in black had a thick head of curly dark hair and a bushy mustache he kept stroking. He wore a big black ring on the middle finger of both hands and a necklace made of what looked like human teeth. Sensing that he was being watched, the man turned and stared at Denny, who glanced away again.

After several minutes of consultation, the judge announced, "The twin seers of Orynca agree that we need to extradite the prisoner. Bailiffs, prepare him for transport."

The wooden witness box flew to the ground and the bars fell away. The dreaded, most fearsome pirate to trawl the American seas screamed like a girl as the bailiff fairies each grabbed an arm and took him away.

"I want to make it clear that technically speaking, since he has been cursed, Mr. deGacy is one of us, but we have never impeded another court's justice," the judge said.

Howard deGacy's shrieks could still be heard from outside the courtroom. It was profoundly disturbing.

Wonder what they'll make of his eagle head and wing.

The judge swiveled around to look at Denny. "The curse will be removed before he is transported to the U.S."

Denny nodded. Boy, he really did have to be careful with his thoughts around here.

"You can enter the witness box," the judge informed him. "I'm keen to hear your story."

"But, your honor, my case is number three," Denny responded.

"And I'm making it number two. Get in. *Now.*"

Denny's breath caught in his throat and he took the

witness stand. *This is worse than walking the plank.* He glanced downward, half expecting to see a pool of swarming sharks beneath him. Nothing. Just the plush, black carpet.

As Ebba stood and began talking to the judge, Denny thought about his life of crime.

Had it been worth it? He wasn't sure about that. Except for meeting Merritt. Denny remembered that the prince was supposed to be here but saw no sign of him. He scanned the room from top to bottom, surprised to see winged creatures fluttering high in the ceiling.

"State your name for the court," the judge boomed.

"Denny, or Dunstan Derrick. But I go by Denny Derrick Dalton, sir."

Some twittering among the jurors.

"Delusions of grandeur with three names?" the judge asked.

"Not anymore, your honor."

Scattered laughter in the courtroom.

"Proceed," the judge said, his lips seeming to move into a half smile. He focused on Denny as though the gossip around him wasn't taking place.

Ebba cleared her throat. "Until a few months ago, Denny Derrick Dalton was the most feared pirate on the high seas."

Denny tried not to stick out his chest with pride.

"He took pleasure in his fearsome reputation, most of it well earned, since he'd worked so hard at being very, very bad."

All eyes stared up at him. Denny saw surprise in many gazes and knew his fairy wings had ruined his scary look.

"He had a difficult childhood. Born in East London in 1816, Denny was taught pickpocketing and thievery by his mother, Mrs. Mable-Anne Dalton. She would hit him until he became fearless about extracting money, with menaces and a flick knife."

Denny's cheeks burned. How did she know all of this? His background was his private shame. He'd hated his mother then and hated her now.

83

"Mable-Anne was a scary, shady character. She started beating her youngest child, Denny's sister, Polly, who was seven, two years younger than Denny. He took Polly's beatings for her. Things went from bad to worse when Denny's dad left them for another woman—"

How does she know all this?

"And left Denny to care for his sister. His mother was never around, but Denny worked honestly as a chimney sweep." She paused with a dramatic inhale. "And his father frequently beat him for those funds."

Ebba stopped reading from her notes and gazed, sad-eyed around the court.

Denny's ears went red. He could feel it. People were staring at him with pity.

"Mable-Anne got caught stealing an onion and was sent to Botany Bay, Australia," Ebba continued. "Denny's father received a note from her several months later saying that the women on these ships were used as whores.

"'It's a floatin', bleedin' bloody brothel,' she wrote. Last heard, Mable-Anne and her common-law husband, another convict she'd met on the ship, had stolen the Australian governor's eight-oared long boat, and escaped the prison island."

Denny was stunned. Why had he heard none of this? He leaned forward, keen to hear more.

"Nobody has heard from them since," Ebba reported, "but there is a bounty on their heads."

"Is there any news of my sister?" Denny asked, his voice cracking. "I've searched the world for her!"

There was a murmur in the court, stricken gazes cast in his direction. Denny knew he'd made a terrible mistake. It would be the gallows for him, for sure.

The judge banged his gavel. "Order! Order! The prisoner will refrain from idle chit-chat with the prosecution."

Denny's hackles rose. "It's not idle chit-chat. I've lost my sister!"

"Shut up!" the judge boomed.

84

The crowd gasped.

"Yes, your honor." Denny shrank back in his seat. He received an evil glare from Ebba, who then continued.

"Denny's father fell apart then, drinking and not paying his debts. His girlfriend left him and he spent most of his time in the pub, but had something of a home with his children. When Denny was ten, he and his father and sister entered a workhouse, where they were given horrible jobs. Denny picked oakum and frequently did his sister's share of the work, too. Their father ground up human bones for fertilizer."

A gasp went up around the courtroom, which seemed to put a gleam in Ebba's eye.

"When they were released almost a year later, Denny and Polly were left to their own devices. They hardly saw their father after that. He'd taken over a pub in Westminster with the new woman in his life."

Ebba held Denny's gaze when she said, "His father was often heard to be saying he had no son.

"Denny took work in a cotton factory and the long hours meant he rarely saw Polly. He was eleven, she was almost nine, but Polly was too young by law to be put to work in a factory. Denny paid a family that had taken over his father's rented apartment to look after Polly, but when he went to find her she was gone.

"They told him she'd been arrested for stealing and that a British military officer had adopted her and taken her to Australia to be with his own family. Denny was determined to travel to Botany Bay to find her, but by the time he was old enough to procure work that would take him away from East London, none of the ships traveled that far. He started life honestly as a rigger on a ferry sailing from Dover to Calais, in France. He soon realized there was no money, but plenty of calluses in that way of life.

"He took on a bigger ship traveling to Spain, and after being attacked by pirates, he realized he had to become one, too. A yo, ho, ho and a bottle of rum were the ideal life for him. He was arrested in the Spanish islands for drinking, along with senior crewmen. He was sexually assaulted there by the head jailer, a personal sacrifice that his crewmembers never forgot. When he mutinied and took over the ship two years later, not a single crewmember left him."

There was a deathly silence, and Denny wondered how his later exploits would be viewed. He blocked all thoughts of Christoph, for fear the judge and jury would read his mind.

"When you took over the ship and renamed her the La-Di-Da, what kind of activities did you engage in?" Ebba asked him.

Good one. Be direct. Merciless. "Pirating activities," Denny replied.

A small titter in the courtroom.

"You switched your normal course of the Indian Ocean to the North Atlantic Ocean. Can you explain why?"

Oh, I get what she's doing now. Denny adopted his most serious expression and said, "I had observed that shipping traffic between Africa, the Caribbean, and Europe began to soar and that in spite of changes in the law regarding slavery, some ships still trafficked slaves bound for Europe and the Caribbean. My crew and I rescued hundreds of slaves and delivered them back to their island homes. You were one of the people we saved."

The room erupted in a stampede of applause and excited chatter.

"Silence!" the judge shouted. The room fell quiet again.

"We have a witness for the prosecution," one of the Unseelie Court fairies said, poking her tongue out at Denny. He stared at her. *Charming. Very mature.*

"Who is it?" the judge asked.

"My brother," Ebba replied. She looked devastated. "Captain Denny rescued both of us."

"He raped me!" Larks shrieked, running down the stairs. None of the fairies tried to touch him. They all edged away as he roared down toward the bench. Larks seemed to know exactly where to stand and took his place beside Pegasus.

"Is this true?" the judge asked Denny.

"No. I admit we had intimacy, many times in fact." He glanced down at Larks. "But he loved everything we did together."

"It's not true!" Larks jumped up and down like a demented flea. "I love women. He had to restrain me to have sex with me."

"Is he telling the truth?" the judge asked.

"We used restraints, but he liked it. He asked me to do it." Denny experienced a fluttering sensation deep within him.

Merritt is here.

Denny could feel it. He held his breath and looked around. *Where is he?*

"It's not true. I love women!" Larks was going crazy, punching the air with his balled-up fists and kicking some unseen assailant.

The entire courtroom fell silent as he screamed, "Don't touch me. Get your hands off me!"

"What's going on?" the judge asked.

"It's a spiritual malady, your honor," Ebba said. "Ever since he went to see a witch doctor in Honduras, my brother has been afflicted by nighttime terrors." She cast an accusatory glance at Denny. "This was right after my client made him walk the plank. Most people don't survive. Those that do are often haunted by it. Larks tried to get help." She paused and thrust her hands dramatically toward her brother who now rolled around the floor, muttering in some strange tongue, his eyes rolling back in his head. "And now look at him!"

Oh, my God. Why is she doing this to me? She's supposed to be defending me, not handing my head on a platter to the jury. Denny and everybody else stared at Larks. Some people stood to get a better view. Some seemed traumatized. Others gave Denny fierce looks. Some people grinned and shook their heads.

The judge conferred with the twin seers, and on the far end of the bench, Denny caught the gaze of a very old black man who watched him through a telescope.

"Bailiff, take the witness away if he can't behave in the courtroom," the judge suddenly said.

Larks' shaking and muttering intensified as a black fairy came for him.

She had trouble holding onto Larks. The judge shouted at Denny over the disturbance.

"Why did you make him walk the plank?"

Denny glanced at Ebba. "Do I have to tell him?"

"Of course you do." She looked worried, though. "You have to tell," she said, obviously realizing for the first time that Denny might have had a good reason to banish her brother.

"Answer the question!" the judge boomed.

"Your honor." Denny's voice squeaked, his throat hoarse and dry. "We had just delivered almost all of the slaves we freed to the Canary Islands. Ebba wanted to go home, but since my crew and I were heading to Europe, Larks wanted to stay on board."

Larks sat up, spewed green bile and a second black fairy arrived and helped the struggling bailiff with him. The room took on a foul odor. Some began to cough and hack, but Denny pressed on.

"We had a cat aboard the ship named Theodore, your honor. He was a fantastic cat. I discovered that Larks wasn't feeding him. In fact, Theodore was starving. I commanded Larks to feed him and he refused. Nobody starves on my ship," Denny finished, his eyes watering badly. "Nobody."

A gasp went up in the courtroom. People started yelling and getting to their feet. Denny had no idea if they were mad at him or Larks, and became frightened when they chanted, "Hang him! Hang him!"

His blood seemed to freeze in his veins and he had frightening visions of being dragged from the witness box straight to the gallows.

Larks laughed and vomited more putrid stuff. The bailiffs finally carried him out of the room, as he twitched and jerked in their arms.

"Court will adjourn for one hour to clear the room," the judge said. "And somebody get the crying pirate out of that box."

"I'm not crying," Denny sniveled. "Someone's been cutting onions." Indeed, the stench that followed Larks' spectacular purging smelled strongly of onions, and Denny, being so close to him, had copped the brunt of it. Even poor Pegasus kept shaking his head and whinnying.

A couple of Unseelie Fairies came and got Denny. Fairies everywhere were touching him as the bars fell away and myriad tiny hands lifted him out of the box. One fairy even grabbed his cock and balls and squeezed.

"What the…" Denny had never met such slutty fairies in his life.

"Thank you," one of them whispered in his ear over the din in the courtroom. "Cats are fairies' friends. They protect us from the monkeys." She plopped a big kiss on Denny's cheek. What monkeys? What was she talking about? The fairies lifted him high and soared out of the courtroom with him, back down the corridor, over the moat and into his cell again.

Alone once more, he fell on the bed and closed his eyes. He felt awful after the onion-like stench of Larks' vomit. He went over the events of his trial so far and wondered if he was losing or winning, the will to live that is. He knew now he could never return to piracy. He was a marked man. His wings guaranteed he'd never be accepted by humans and he had no other skills, though in his one and only week at school when he was five, he'd showed remarkable aptitude for finger painting. Perhaps he could take up a career of painting. Or he could write his memoirs.

After all, he had a tale to tell, didn't he?

He recalled the British botanist and explorer Allan

Cunningham, who he'd met four years ago at the seaport of Southampton, England. Cunningham had been heading back to Australia, where he'd spent many happy years collecting plant specimens. Cunningham was obsessed with the place and had been busy writing scientific papers, some of which Denny had read. He'd been taught to read by some of his ship's officers and had almost regretted this ability when he'd clapped eyes on Cunningham's dreary jottings. But still. If Cunningham could find an audience for his work, surely Denny could attract a few readers with his wild sea tales?

The idea took flight in his mind and he hoped that he could live long enough to tell his tale. The lock of his cell jangled, and he sprang up on the bed just as Ebba entered, carrying a tray loaded with food and drink. In spite of the fact that he felt she'd thrown him to the wolves, the smell of the chicken stew made his stomach rumble. She placed the tray on the desk.

"I'm sorry about what I said," she told him, eyes downcast. "I brought you nectar to make up for it."

"That's okay." It surprised him how congenial he could sound when several minutes ago he'd wanted to kill her.

"I knew the court would be thrilled at the reason you made my brother walk the plank but the fact remains, you still made him do it."

"Yes, I understand." He rushed to the table and had the first taste of stew in his mouth before he'd even taken a seat.

She began to pace as Denny ate. The bread on his tray had been slightly toasted, which gave it a good crunch. His toes curled with pleasure inside his moccasins. This was the stuff of dreams. He picked up the goblet and drank the silky, golden liquid, feeling wonderful. Why did she look so worried?

"What's going on?" he asked, wiping his mouth with the back of his hand.

"We had a good beginning but I'm anxious about the next part of the trial. I am going to try to focus on the shipping and trading part and less on the pillaging and plundering." She frowned. "They'll want to know about the ship's captain, Lester Piggins, and the mutiny and the men you've killed."

The door to the cell rattled, and the green-winged fairy appeared. "Ebba. You're wanted in the courtroom." He gave Denny a swift glance. "Enjoy your supper. It may be your last."

"Don't worry," Denny said, waving a piece of bread around, "I will."

Ebba looked alarmed as she followed the green-winged fairy out of the cell. She had a lot riding on this case. And so did Denny. He kept thinking about the prince and wondered if he really had been in the courtroom. *Or did I imagine it?* He was certain he hadn't and, when he closed his eyes and really concentrated, felt sure he'd been up in the rafters with many winged creatures. *I'll look for him when I go back.* When Denny got back to the courtroom he'd take his time and watch. He knew he would find his prince.

After he'd eaten his last bite of food and licked the nectar cup clean, he lay on his bed and daydreamed about Merritt. His thoughts took him back to the day he had captured a ship heading for San Juan, Puerto Rico. For two years he had coveted the fabrics and rum aboard the Clementine. He had seen the ship many times in various ports and would have known her anywhere. He'd been surprised to see her way off course, but when he'd studied the ship through a telescope, he'd realized quickly that the ship had already been overtaken and renamed the Charlotte.

* * * *

The high seas

Seventeen months earlier…
Denny and Rigby spent time watching a drunken pirate crew carousing on deck.

"Who is it?" Rigby asked.

91

Denny had a suspicion it was Lewis Horton, a British sailor turned pirate. He was famous for taking prisoners and starving them to death. He would force them to do embarrassing things in the form of games for a mere crust of bread.

"Horton, I think." Denny was more determined than ever to capture the ship and possibly eliminate the vile Horton from the world of men.

"Really?" Rigby sucked in a breath and took the spyglass from Denny's hands. He watched the singing, dancing crew a few moments and said, "Aye, it's him. That weasel. I'd recognize those ginger curls anywhere, not to mention that stupid chicken dance he's so fond of."

"There's a woman on board," Denny muttered, releasing a sigh. He was certain he could see her crying.

Although he sexually favored men, he loved women and strove to protect them, especially if they were young. He wanted to rescue them all, because it ate at him that he'd been unable to save Polly. One day he would sail to Australia and find her. In the meantime, he would have to wait until one of the seamen he'd bribed into helping him sent him news of her situation. He had various men who'd been well paid to search for her, with promises of more money once they learned something. He'd also offered an extra, huge reward to any man who brought her back to Denny. Alive, of course. Each time he arrived at a new port, he checked with the clerks there for news. He'd never had any.

"Oh, yeah. I see the woman now. Her feet are bound," Rigby murmured. "They're making her kick a ball around the deck but of course she keeps falling."

"Fire the cannons!" Denny shouted.

Things happened quickly after that. Denny and his crew climbed aboard and soon learned that the Charlotte's pirate crew had been helping themselves to the stores of rum for weeks. It showed in the way they indiscriminately fired their weapons, even shooting at one another as Denny's crew came up alongside the vessel and climbed on board.

Horton fired at his female captive but missed. She screamed as the bullet grazed her shoulder then lodged in the deck. The Charlotte was sinking as the battle raged between the two pirate crews. Horton fired at the woman again but Denny shot him in the hand. He collapsed on the deck where Rigby finished him with a shot to the head. The woman kept screaming, and Denny picked her up, attempting to carry her off the ship and onto the La-Di-Da.

"It's for your own protection. We won't hurt you, I can promise you that," he yelled over her constant shrieks.

"My brother's below deck. He's in bad shape. They've kept him in shackles for weeks."

"I'll get him," Denny promised. He delivered her to the deck of the La-Di-Da and hastened back to the Charlotte. With his bosun, Woodruff, at his heels, Denny scoured the ship until he followed the sounds of faint moaning and found a young man, half conscious and chained to the wall in the stowage. Both Woodruff and Denny were horrified by the man's inhumane conditions. The stench of piss, feces and vomit was strong, and Denny had to hold his breath as he helped lift the near-skeletal creature.

"Shoot me. Please kill me," the man begged, his fetid breath almost knocking out Denny. His blue eyes stared at him from beneath ragged, crusted eyelashes, but Denny ignored him and carried the man in his soiled clothing off the ship and onto his own. He couldn't believe how light the man was, and the protruding bones emerging from his ripped clothing looked damaged and bruised.

Denny carried him to the ship's sickbay. "He's been beaten," Denny murmured as he and Woodruff stripped him of his disgusting clothing. The young man couldn't sit or speak but seemed to understand questions. His breath came in putrid gasps.

"What is his name?" Denny glanced at the young man's sister.

She ignored Denny the first few times he asked. She

had come aboard with them and kept close, pacing and wringing her hands. The woman hovered over her brother as though Denny might snap every bone in his body.

"Careful," she kept saying. "Think of him as precious cargo."

No. I was thinking of him as dinner. Denny's thoughts raged. Wasn't it obvious he was helping her brother? "Get the surgeon," Denny instructed Woodruff.

Woodruff retreated and soon returned with Arthur Fellows, the best ship's doctor Denny had ever worked with in his seafaring career.

Woodruff beckoned Denny aside. "I'm scouting for survivors. Only four deaths." Woodruff was a kindly man for a pirate. Big-hearted and, well, big all over, even his whisper sounded like an exploding cannon.

"None of our own have perished?" Denny asked, concerned.

"None, sir. Couple of injuries. Pride wounded more than anything, but one of the pirates from the Charlotte is missing."

The patient stirred. Denny lowered his voice. "Which one?"

"They say it's a rough lad named Scruggs." The oblivious Woodruff kept booming as he went on. "They say he was responsible for this. Got a real mean streak in him." Woodruff gestured to the patient, who became agitated at the mere mention of Scruggs' name.

His sister knelt beside him, soothing him.

Woodruff pulled Denny outside the room and managed to drop his voice to report, "We found two dead bodies in the same room we found our patient."

"Go. Keep me informed." Denny had never felt so angry or helpless. Suddenly, early retirement in Cornwall seemed very appealing. Denny had never seen the point in killing for its own sake, especially in such a cruel, inexplicable way.

Woodruff left, and Denny returned to the sickbay, where he and the woman stood by as Fellows examined the patient.

Denny stole a couple of looks at her. She was thin, but not underfed. Her eyes were pale brown. Hazel, Denny thought they called it. Her long hair was dirty and matted, but must have shone like spun gold when it was clean. He glanced at her brother. As long as he lived, Denny would never forget the frightened-cow eyes of the starving young man as Fellows examined him.

When Denny asked the woman once again for her brother's name, her face looked like a volcano on the verge of eruption. Several moments went by before she said, "Merritt," as though giving up some huge secret. The surgeon looked up at them.

"Kindly fetch boiling water. And Denny, bring me my medical supplies."

Denny went and got the kettle from the galley, clean towels and sponges, and a large bowl. He grabbed a cake of plain white soap and dashed back to the sickbay. Fellows kept examining Merritt as his sister gently bathed him with the sponges and bucket after bucket of hot, soapy water. Merritt looked a bit better but the smell of rotting flesh didn't leave him.

"He has been beaten," Fellows whispered to Denny. "Woodruff mentioned to me that you observed this and it's true. But some of the bruising and marks are scurvy. Obviously he is suffering severe malnutrition and advanced scurvy." He pointed to the dark spots all over Merritt's arms and legs and raised his voice. "His severe lack of vitamins has affected him tremendously. We can help him recover quickly with fresh sweet peppers. We have a supply of capsicums on board. Fresh fruit would help." He paused. "Tropical fruit and broccoli. We have some of both." He glanced at Denny, inclining his head. "We will discuss more privately."

They took a moment to walk outside. Fellows looked shaken. "He was sodomized and has not healed well. I think it's more than I can handle."

Silence fell between them, and Denny swallowed. "Is that the smell?"

"Yes. He does not seem in pain, but there is some sort of anal fissure, which explains the smell. I'd like to suggest a treatment of leeches."

"Absolutely not." Denny had never approved of the method of putting blood-sucking worms on a man's skin. "He doesn't have any blood clots that I can see." Blood-letting would surely kill poor Merritt faster than allowing him to rest and heal.

Fellows looked disappointed. "My leeches won't survive if I don't give them fresh blood soon." He cast a hopeful glance at Denny, who shook his head.

"Don't look at me. I hate bloody leeches!"

He returned to Merritt, whose gaze kept flicking around the sickbay. He let out a gasp when Denny left a few minutes later, as though he wanted to speak but couldn't. Denny quickly returned with some of his own clean nightclothes out of his cabin. He helped the woman dress Merritt.

"Food," Denny muttered. "I'll get him some."

"No!" she commanded, looking terrified. What was going on? Was it just their recent captivity, or something else?

"You're safe here," he assured her. "Nobody will hurt your brother anymore. Not on my ship."

She didn't seem convinced.

"Where are you from?"

"Soriano," she responded, her eyes downcast.

"I've never heard of it."

"It's a small volcanic island off the coast of Honduras. Not many people have heard of it." She lifted her head and her defiant gaze made her eyes seem black. She blinked and they were a warm chocolate brown.

He'd been sure her eyes were blue but maybe he was wrong. It had been a weird day, after all.

"And what is your name?" he asked.

"What is *your* name?" she retorted, her tone prim.

"Captain Denny Derrick Dalton. At your service."

"My name is Fortunata." She looked at him as though expecting him to know of her name, then gripped his hand with a fierce shake of her slim fingers.

He almost screamed in pain when a couple of his bones cracked. She didn't break them but he was certain she could crumble rocks with those frightening digits.

"Okay," he said, breathing through the surge of agony. "If you would like to supervise the cooking, I'm sure the cook won't mind."

Ebba and her brother Larks had left the ship a few weeks before, and though Denny had adored Ebba's cooking, he knew she would never have tolerated Fortunata's scrutiny.

Merritt's sister disappeared then returned twenty minutes later with a beef stew Merritt took in small, hesitant bites. He also nibbled at the strips of red capsicum that she fed him. He fell back against his pillows after a few spoonfuls, as though the effort had cost him. And it probably had. Denny had never seen somebody in such a bad state. Fellows told him later that day that Merritt would have been dead within two days had help not arrived. The crew of the La-Di-Da found the missing pirate floating out at sea. He had taken a barrel of rum from the Charlotte's stocks but had somehow drowned. Denny's men brought the barrel aboard and left Scruggs out there, lifelessly floating in the water.

Denny didn't know how the man had died and didn't care. He, like Fortunata and Fellows, worried about Merritt's shut-down condition. Over the next two days, various crewmembers sat with Merritt so he was never alone. Somehow, he improved dramatically. One evening, Denny went to visit him with a bowl of stew that included the remains of the Italian pasta they'd traded with a Sardinian ship docked in Nantes, France.

Merritt seemed to like the small, toasted balls of pasta called fregula. For the first time, Denny and Merritt talked. Merritt's cheeks were filling in and he laughed at Denny's pronunciation of fregula. He'd said Freg-you-la.

Merritt's eyes danced with amusement as he said, "It's

freg-oola."

Denny laughed too. He didn't feel mocked. He was certain Merritt liked him. The young man was recuperating faster than Denny had expected, but Fellows had advised him that with constant helpings of fresh fruit and sweet peppers, Merritt could regain much of his strength and gain significant health within a few weeks.

This both pleased and devastated Denny. He knew Fellows wanted to take Merritt to the local hospital in San Juan, the Puerto Rican port that, weather permitting, they would reach in about three weeks. Denny wanted Merritt to regain his health and his masculine confidence but he feared losing the one man he felt he could talk to. Denny knew he was setting himself up for a collision course with disaster because he was falling in love. Merritt became his focus, and his joy. Minutes with him became precious. He adored every second with the magnificent young man whose gaining vitality revealed a little more of the vibrant, handsome Merritt really was.

Denny never spoke of his rising feelings for Merritt. He cradled his love within, like a mother hen protecting a hard-laid egg. He had never felt such tenderness or such incredible passion for another man. It took Denny another week to realize his feelings were being returned. And one person was acutely aware and not at all pleased. His frosty, controlling sister, Fortunata. Sometimes Denny caught her looking at him in a way that made her seem more fearsome than even the strongest, most homicidal men he'd encountered on the high seas.

And yet, she was beautiful, and could be charming when she chose to be so.

I don't trust her. I have a horrible feeling she could be the death of me.

Chapter Seven

Merritt sat against a rock eating an apple picked from a tree on the outskirts of Gremma's property. Now that his faculties were returning to him he could see the almost invisible, shimmery web that she or, more likely, Fortunata had cast on the ground and trees. He doubted it was the work of Gremma because she'd been surprised to find Cillian lying dead on the ground.

"But there is nothing here that would ever harm an animal," she'd told Fortunata.

Now that he saw the invisible force field, Merritt knew his favorite horse's death had not been the result of poisoning. The apple Elvin had given Merritt hadn't been tainted and the cut inflicted on Cillian hadn't led to his death. The force field had killed him, but what evil, potent magic had been in it to inflict such harm? He sighed, relieved at least that Elvin hadn't plotted Merritt's death.

Fortified once more, Merritt moved forward, determined to grab the cloak, confront Gremma and finally end his sister's cruel practices. He swayed suddenly and blinked.

It's Denny. I think he's here. The knowledge both pleased and frightened him. Denny was close. They'd been so far apart, and yet, he would go on trial, and with the bizarre jury running the court these days he could hang before nightfall, or be kept in leg irons for months.

He hurried toward Gremma's house. He flicked a hand toward the bewitched land but nothing moved. *Still cursed. Damn. I need the cloak. I must tear it apart to destroy its power.* Merritt took a few more steps and heard ragged sobs. Following the sound, he took care to be quiet. Merritt was stunned when he saw Gremma sitting, sprawled on the ground, examining her face in a green, handheld mirror. She looked even more decrepit, and older than she had the day before, but in the mirror, she was young and beautiful again.

"Merritt," she breathed, lifting a tearstained face up to him.

"Gremma." In spite of all that had happened between them, in spite of all the rotten things she'd done over the years, he pitied her. "I can save you."

Her eyes shone, tears still leaking down her face.

"But you must do everything I tell you to do, and when it's done, you must leave this island."

"Leave?" She looked shocked.

"Leave," he repeated. "Forever."

She looked surprised, then wary and angry. Another wart sprouted on her hand. She gave a little shriek. "I'll do it. I'll do whatever you say, only make this stop," she begged.

"Where is my sister?" he asked, dropping beside Gremma.

"I haven't seen her. She disappeared yesterday, and then this happened." She dropped the mirror in her lap and opened the top button of the coat she was wearing. Oozing, green sores appeared all over her neck. "Are you sure you can save me?"

Lightning crackled overhead.

Merritt glanced up at the sky and smiled. "I think my sister just realized your magic is not only failing, but coming back to hurt her. Twofold."

* * * *

The La-Di-Da

A year earlier…

Denny wasn't sure when Fortunata first became aware of the growing, gentle romance between Denny and Merritt, but he was convinced that she sensed it. She took to making sure the two men had little time alone together. The few private moments they shared were spent uttering words and sharing kisses Denny had never exchanged with anyone, especially another man. He'd had plenty of sex, but had never dared lay his soul bare with another. The times he and Merritt were together and unable to touch were agony for both of them. As soon as Fortunata or whoever was with them would leave, Merritt would whisper, "Kiss me, please."

His hands would shake and his lips would tremble as they shared soul embraces Denny had never dreamed were possible. He began to have vivid dreams of a life he'd never allowed himself, a kind of happiness he'd imagined would always be denied him because of his sexual preferences. He made no secret of his homosexuality, but didn't flaunt it either.

They'd been at sea two weeks when Merritt started walking on deck. His first attempts were pathetic, by his own admission. Denny admired his sense of humor and determination. The entire crew was stunned by his marked improvements.

"I'm a better doctor than I thought," Fellows kept telling everyone.

Whenever he went on this way, Fortunata glared at him. Denny put it down to sheer possessiveness. She loved Merritt with such an obsession that it continued to scare Denny. When she would turn around and be sweet to him again, he'd experience extreme feelings of guilt for being suspicious of her.

As the days went by and Merritt grew stronger, he wanted to help with ship duties. Nobody would let him, but everybody admired his fighting spirit. It turned out he was an expert mapmaker, but told Denny that when the boat he'd shared with his sister and two cousins had been hijacked, all his maps and tools had been destroyed.

Denny showed him a map of the Caribbean, hoping Merritt could show him his island home off the coast of Honduras. Merritt just smiled. "It's not on any map," he said, not even glancing at Denny's well-marked papers. "But trust me, it's there. Doriana is a paradise."

Denny stared at him. Fortunata had called the island Soriano, but Merritt called it Doriana. Were they both... cuckoo? Or had Denny misheard her the first time Fortunata mentioned it?

He leaned toward the latter. After all, they'd been under extreme survival conditions and the two names were close. Weren't they? And yet, questions persisted and niggled at him.

Merritt was a hearty eater who endured plates of raw peppers and slightly cooked broccoli with a stoic air. Fellows had done some research in the musty old textbooks he'd inherited when the crew had taken over the ship. He told Denny and Merritt that doctors prescribed the addition of fried seal meat to a scurvy patient's diet, but the idea horrified both Merritt and Denny.

"I'm fine with everything I'm already eating. Honest!" Merritt insisted.

"But seals are delicious," Fellows said, clearly disappointed. He gave Denny a bleak look that might have said, 'First no leeches. Now this.'

With Merritt's improved health, shipboard dinners became entertaining affairs with different crewmembers performing each night. Fortunata had a wonderful voice and sang beautiful, haunting love songs, but nothing beat Merritt's plaintive *Oh, Tell Me How from Love to Fly*. Denny thought he was listening to an angel.

"*Oh, tell me how from love to fly, its dangers how to shun. To guard the heart, to shield the eye, or I must be undone!*" Merritt sang the lyrics with a soul-tearing heartbreak that left everyone silent. He seemed to be staring right at Denny, who glanced away when Fortunata narrowed her gaze and glared at him.

Rigby was in the mood for laughter and began singing the rousing chorus from *Drunken Sailor*. He would have gone on until morning screaming, "*What shall we do with the drunken sailor?"* over and over again. He would have knocked back more shots of rum, had he not got kicked by one of the crewmen and keeled over in the midst of laughter. He had then fallen into a merciful, silent sleep. Denny and Fellows carried him to his cabin, Merritt and Fortunata right behind them. From the sounds of muted laugher, the others had continued drinking in comparative quiet.

"Is he always like that?" Fortunata asked with a haughty air, staring daggers at the snoozing Rigby.

"One sniff of the barmaid's skirt and he's impossible." Fellows rolled his eyes.

"Well, we wish you goodnight," Fortunata responded.

Merritt echoed her words, his gaze fastened on Denny. His sister pulled him by the arm, leading him away. Denny and Fellows paused for breath. Fellows huffed as they dragged Rigby to the quarterdeck, where he lived with the other ship's officers.

As they pulled off Rigby's boots and outer garments, Rigby unleashed a sort of mad giggle and sang, *"What do we do with..."* before falling asleep again in the middle of the chorus.

"Is it just me or does he pong?" Fellows' nose twitched.

"Aye, he needs a bath," Denny agreed, sliding into an immediate panic.

Fellows scrunched his nose and gave a shudder. "How does he breathe in his own fumes?"

Denny shrugged, privately fretting. What if he himself needed a bath? He raced to his cabin to bathe before going to visit Merritt to wish him a goodnight. Cold water and soap from a basin was a small improvement, especially when he rinsed out the water three times until it almost ran clear, but he felt he needed something more, especially since he was putting back on the same clothing. He tiptoed back to Rigby's cabin where his second mate was snoring in bed like a hibernating bear. Denny borrowed Rigby's proudest purloined item in life, a bottle of the French perfumer Farina's *Eau de Cologne*. It had belonged to a British officer whose private quarters had been ransacked by Denny and his crew when his sloop had been moored at the Port of Antwerp in Belgium.

The cologne had a distinctive, pungent scent. People said that Napoleon loved the stuff. *Wait. He didn't exactly have a happy ending…* As Denny dabbed a bit on his face and under his armpits, worried thoughts crossed his mind. *Yeah, but look what happened to him.* People also said the cologne came from the town where the water was supposed to be strong enough to ward off the bubonic plague. *I hope so. Not that I'm expecting to get that any time soon. Not getting bitten by any rats today, thank you…*

He returned the bottle to Rigby's cabin then went back to his own quarters, checking his appearance in the cracked hand mirror he'd pinched in the raid on the British sloop. Denny thought he looked okay, though his head itched something fierce. Then his chin prickled. Denny scratched at it, dismayed because it seemed that the finer things in life just weren't meant for him. The sensation grew worse so he washed his face and head, his hair still dripping a little as he went off to visit Merritt.

Merritt was still sleeping in the sickbay even though he had most of his meals with the others. He lay in bed staring up at the ceiling, bolting upward when Denny entered the room.

"She's coming back," Merritt whispered. He sniffed the air. "What's that smell?" His eyes widened. "Why did you come here wearing cologne? You can't even kiss me now. She'll know!" The desolate expression on his face did more for Denny's self-esteem than all the kisses in the world.

He likes me. He really does. Denny did an inward jig. "'Tis no matter. I wanted to see you. Where did she go?"

Merritt kept sniffing. "You've bathed." He looked surprised.

"Um, yeah." Denny frowned. *Boy, I must have needed it worse than I thought.*

Merritt plumped up his pillows so that he was half sitting

and half lying back on his bunk. "She's in her cabin mixing some herbal concoction for me. They always taste terrible but they do work."

Denny was afraid to ask what was in these concoctions and he hoped she wasn't planning on coming back anytime soon, but seconds later she was there. She smiled when she saw that Denny was nowhere near her brother.

"Ah, Captain," she said, her tone a warm purr. *Boy, does she know how to manipulate and charm me. Calling me captain...* "I would have brought you a tonic had I known you'd be here." She turned to her brother. "Drink up, darling. This will soothe your liver."

Merritt sat up straighter and took the cup she offered him. Denny stared at it. It looked as though it was made of gold. Where had she found it? She'd come on board the La-Di-Da with nothing. Or had she? *I have to get into her cabin and look at the stuff she's using to mix her potions.*

Denny loitered for a few minutes but finally excused himself. He returned to his cabin, exhausted. Stripping off most of his clothes, he kept his vest and undergarments on then threw himself into bed. The ship's cat, Theodore, came out from under the bed and joined him. Denny loved that cat more than anyone or anything else in the world, except Merritt, and he let the orange tabby snuggle beside him. Theodore was a funny cat. He wasn't particularly affectionate but liked snuggling and would purr for half an hour upon close contact with Denny. *I think I do the same thing with Merritt, come to think of it.*

Within minutes, Denny was asleep but also aware of strange, unsettling dreams that left him restless in bed. He was aware of the cabin door opening and, unable to open his eyes for some reason, realized it was Merritt getting into bed with him. Theodore was not pleased, but soon, with Merritt stroking his fur, the cat purred loudly. The sound would have been a fine early-warning alarm.

"He never lets me touch him," Denny murmured, trying hard to rouse himself awake, but he couldn't.

Merritt chuckled then leaned across the cat and kissed Denny's cheek. He spooned Denny, rubbed his head until Denny fell asleep, the cat kept purring between them.

Denny had the most beautiful dreams of his life but awakened early only to find Merritt and the cat leaving the cabin. Denny couldn't say anything about Merritt. He was obviously worried about his sister finding his empty bed. But the cat! What a little traitor! Denny got out of bed and, for the first time ever aboard ship, took stock of his dirty clothes and realized all of them were filthy. His biggest single regret had been to eliminate the laundry detail on board the La-Di-Da. It had become everybody's personal responsibility to care for their own clothing. Some of the crew liked to drag their clothes through the ocean water, or wait for the times they docked in port. They were running low on everything, including tanks of water, so they couldn't arrive in Puerto Rico soon enough, except... If Merritt and his sister left the ship, as was Fortunata's plan, then Denny would never see him again.

He swallowed over the lump in his throat and scratched his head. He'd been all right through the night, but now the itching was worse. He tugged at his scalp and felt something moving. He jumped in fright when a knock came at the door.

"Yes?" he called out.

It was Sorenson. He entered the cabin, rubbing at his own head. "Sorry, sir, but Arthur Fellows wants to see you. He says we have a bad case of nits on board and everyone needs their head shaved."

"Thank you," Denny said. *Nits*. Well. It was better than the plague. Up on the deck, Denny found everyone shaving each other's heads. The only one who wouldn't submit was Fortunata.

"I drink a tonic. I have no nits and neither does my brother," she said, stomping below deck with Merritt in tow.

Nobody said a word and from the apprehensive looks on

everyone's faces, Denny saw that he wasn't the only one who was terrified of her.

Later that day, Denny returned to the laundry to retrieve a few of the things he'd left there to dry. Sorenson and Rigby were there whispering to each other.

"What's going on?" Denny asked them as the two men exchanged dark looks.

"The tanks were near empty this morning and now they're full," Rigby said. "Funny things happen whenever *she's* in a room."

It didn't surprise Denny to hear this. He shrugged. "Well, we are still a few days away from Puerto Rico, so let's not look gift horses in mouths, shall we?"

Neither Rigby nor Sorenson seemed happy, but Denny determined not to start rumors and unpleasantness even if he was beginning to suspect Fortunata of some kind of sorcery. If she practiced her...whatever it was...for the greater good, he could deal with a little magic, as long as she didn't put warts on his nose or boils on his bottom. He had a feeling that in spite of how nice she sometimes could be, she would be the type of person to resort to petty vengeance. And Denny loathed boils and warts.

For two days, Fortunata was so lovely, Denny's worries about her seemed unfounded. He was delighted she was being so nice to him. It made Merritt happy. In fact, Fortunata complimented Denny and even flirted with him. She made him porridge on the third day, and the little black dots decorating the surface turned out to be plump little raisins.

"But where did you get them?" Denny asked, moaning in appreciation as he demolished three bowls of porridge.

"In the galley," she said, which appeared to be astonishing news to Sorenson.

Like every other man on board, however, Sorenson feared Fortunata and said, "I might need a monocle soon. I swear my eyesight's getting worse."

When the La-Di-Da neared the port of San Juan in Puerto

Rico, Merritt jumped overboard with some of the crew and frolicked in the ocean with them. Denny realized Fortunata was wearing a new dress and a ruby-red cloak. He wondered where these had come from but was too afraid of her to ask.

She stood beside Denny, smiling as they watched the men get ready to drop anchor. Out of nowhere, a large reef shark appeared and headed right for Merritt. Quick as a wink, she took her hand out of the folds of her cloak and pointed a finger at the shark. Denny gasped, shocked by the long, withered, crooked talon she used. He blinked and her finger seemed normal again.

Denny shook his head. *I have got to stop imagining things.*

The shark swam away with none of the men in the water aware of the apparent close call. With Denny having to check in with the shipping clerks at the port, and all the things that needed to be replenished, he didn't go ashore straight away. Fellows accompanied Merritt and Fortunata to a local monastery, which had an adjoining hospital. Late in the afternoon, Denny went ashore and checked in with the postal clerk, anxious for any messages regarding his sister. Nothing. Swallowing his disappointment, he went in search of Merritt and Fortunata. He spied Foster, Rigby, and Sorenson drinking at a table outside of a taverna in the Plaza de San José, a popular meeting place for locals and visitors. He waved at them, but they seemed deep in conversation, and it didn't seem like a happy one either. He bumped into Fellows, who appeared to be in a rush. "Just meeting the lads for a drink," he said.

"What about our patient?"

"The doctors gave young Merritt a thorough examination and he received a clean bill of health. Both Merritt and his sister have chosen to stay at the monastery for now. They may or may not join us when we depart on Wednesday."

He must have noticed Denny's shocked expression because he said, "She wants a bath and they have plenty of hot water and soap. Merritt was resting last I looked."

"Okay." Denny felt discouraged. He hated the idea of

leaving them here. Well, Merritt more than Fortunata.

He tried not to feel left out that his crewmembers had not invited him to join them for a drink. A little restless, he went and got a proper shave at one of the many barber shops in the village. He enjoyed being pampered with nice-smelling shave soap and lavender water to soothe and tone the skin afterward. He knew the barber from previous visits to San Juan but never understood a word the man said. He just let him ramble, and lay back in his chair with burning hot towels strewn across his face.

When it was time to leave, Denny was anxious to get back to the ship. He knew only too well what he and his own crew had done on many occasions. Ransacking other moored ships had always seemed like a laugh, but not when it was being done to his vessel. He sat up when the barber removed the towels and patted the lavender water onto his cheeks.

I smell like a Madge, but I guess, since I am one, I shouldn't mind. He counted out a generous stash of gold coins to the barber, whose eyes lit up with joy, and that was when Denny noticed a small boy peering around the entrance of the barbershop. As soon as his gaze connected with Denny's, the child vanished.

How odd. I don't think I know him.

As he walked back to the ship, the little boy kept darting around buildings and finally beckoned to Denny. Denny pointed to his chest as if to ask, 'Me?'

The boy nodded and beckoned to him again. They passed the monastery, where bells rang and male voices lifted in a beautiful, hypnotic chant. Around more corners and up a long, long flight of stairs, Denny followed the child, who entered what looked like a belfry, and there, wearing a long white tunic, stood Merritt, smiling at him.

Denny counted out a generous amount of coins for the child, who looked ecstatic.

"*Gracias, señor!*" he shouted, almost dropping some of the coins. They filled both his hands and it didn't seem as though the boy had any pockets or a purse.

He took off, a smile spearing his face from cheek to cheek.

"I've missed you," Merritt said, disarming Denny.

Denny's ears burned with pleasure and acute embarrassment. "You've only been gone a few hours."

"Longer than that. All day." Merritt sighed. "We don't have much time and I need you."

"I...ah... Oh." Nothing intelligible came out of Denny's mouth. He gratefully accepted Merritt's forthrightness as he stepped forward and claimed Denny's lips in an almost violent kiss that left them both breathless. They broke apart then kissed again, their embrace growing more tender.

"I want to stay with you tonight, but my sister wants me back at the monastery. I promise you we will be on board before your ship leaves." He kissed Denny again. He stepped back and put his hands on Denny's arms. "I want to try something. Do you trust me?"

Denny had no idea what that was supposed to mean. "Trust you with what?"

"Could you bring yourself to trust me?" Merritt repeated.

"I—I think I already do." Denny couldn't deny the passion, the obsession he had for this man. And yes, he did trust him.

Merritt pushed himself away from Denny. He crossed the room and walked over to a large, lacquered wooden cabinet in the far corner. The sun was starting to set, but the light was still pleasant and soft. As he waited, Denny took in his surroundings for the first time. The room was sparse, yet oddly intimate. A large bed with what looked like fresh, crisp white linens stood at one end, a chair beside it, upon which somebody had placed a jar filled with red roses. From somewhere, a faint wind made the thin white curtains billow in the room.

Denny glanced over at Merritt, who approached him again, hands behind his back. "Close your eyes, Denny." His voice was low and husky.

Denny did as he'd been told. He was stunned, but thrilled

110

that Merritt was taking control this way. Merritt came up behind him, his voice as seductive as a feather stroke against Denny's neck and chin.

"Denny." Merritt pressed his body into Denny's, who delighted at the hardness of Merritt's cock against his ass. Merritt placed a tender kiss on Denny's nape then moved around to stand in front of him.

Once again, an eager Denny gave himself up to Merritt's succulent kisses, luxuriating in the way he moved his mouth all over Denny's face. Denny leaned into him, yearning for closer contact. He was hard, so hard for Merritt, whose tongue swept across Denny's lips as he began to undress him.

"You're wearing lavender water. It smells much better," Merritt whispered. "She'll think I stopped at a barber shop."

Denny caught a glimpse of a bundle of silky red rope in Merritt's hand. "What's that?" he asked, reaching for it. He knew, though, just knew before even touching it that it was hemp rope. He'd seen enough of it as a child in the workhouse. He could close his eyes and still feel the coarse strands, but this rope was smooth.

"I hope it's something you'll never forget." Merritt gave him such a dazzling smile, Denny became aroused beyond belief.

Merritt unspooled the rope, taking hold of a length of it. He kissed Denny again, holding his arms up to lower the rope behind Denny's back. Merritt held the rope tight, pulling Denny closer to him. Again he wound the rope around their entwined bodies, bringing them closer still. Then he released the open end and moved behind Denny, whispering, "I am a *nawashi.*"

"What does that mean?" Denny had many fantasies about tying up handsome, captive princes and making mad passionate love to them, but had never even come close to trying it. He'd never even thought about being the one to be tied up. He'd always feared being tied up and not being able to escape if trouble came along. Buggery was, after all,

111

a crime in his own country, but in many other places around the world it seemed more acceptable. And his experiences so far had been fast and furtive. But Merritt, his meek, sweet little Merritt, seemed to have become possessed by some ancient god of lust. His commanding attitude was so alluring Denny feared he might come before Merritt had finished removing his clothes.

Merritt remained behind Denny, making a knot in the rope Denny knew well.

"Some call it a cock's comb," Merritt murmured in his ear.

"Aye. And I know it as a ringbolt hitch. We use it all the time on the ship."

Merritt grunted. "Not like this you don't." He spun Denny around to face him and the knot loosened.

Denny looked down, fascinated to see that the knot had vanished. "What happened? Did you change your mind?" Denny asked, working hard to hide his disappointment.

"I haven't even started with you yet, Captain Dalton." Merritt claimed Denny's mouth once more.

They undressed each other, kicking their shoes off, their lips colliding again. Merritt was as hard as Denny, but when Denny tried to touch him, Merritt pulled back, walking around Denny again.

"I want to introduce you to *kinbaku-bi*, the little-known art of beautiful bondage. I learned all about it from some Japanese sailors." Merritt trailed the bundle of rope along Denny's bare shoulders. "I could inflict pain and torture on you if I choose, but I never will. I want there to be mutual joy, but also the knowledge that we could hurt each other mentally and physically, but we won't."

The expression in his eyes both thrilled and terrified Danny, who swallowed, not sure about any of it, but knowing he wanted to experience this erotic pleasure. Merritt knew some complicated rope-tying. Denny knew some himself and hoped to reciprocate, then remembered what Merritt had been through on the other ship. Gone, however, was the frightened, starving prisoner. This new

112

Merritt was confident and sensual as he nudged Denny into position.

Merritt tied Denny's arms and folded them so that his arms were crossed, his hands resting on his shoulders, as though Denny was praying. He was actually ready to beg for Merritt's touch, and didn't have to wait long for it. Merritt tied Denny tightly enough that Denny couldn't move his hands. It was maddening when he yearned to stroke Merritt's skin.

When Merritt, though, moved his fingers along every crevice of Denny's body then gave Denny's cock and balls a swift swipe with his tongue, Denny broke out in a sweat but could only wiggle back and forth when Merritt pushed him back onto the bed. Merritt wound the rope around Denny's cock and balls, pulled up the binding, making the last knot at a sensitive spot near Denny's groin. It was torture. Delicious, sweet torture. Pain and pleasure flew through Denny's body as Merritt knelt beside him, his cock rigid.

"You see what you do to me?" Merritt reached down and ran his hand along Denny's feverish brow.

"Feeling's mutual," Denny croaked.

Merritt lay beside him, running his hands over Denny's damp body once more. Merritt kept drawing out the pleasure, stroking Denny's tethered cock, kissing him feverishly. Denny pulled against the ropes, anxious for closer contact. Merritt kissed and licked his way down Denny's body, reaching between Denny's legs.

"Oh, yes!" Denny opened his thighs for Merritt's hand, beads of intense sweat peppering his face and chest as Merritt delved first one, then two fingers into Denny's asshole.

Merritt stroked, just a little, letting Denny feel the pressure in his arms again as Merritt picked up the rope leading from Denny's torso to his ball sac. He pulled and tightened the hold. Denny gasped, hardly able to breathe as he silently begged for Merritt to touch his cock again.

Merritt grunted, reaching down and unleashing a long lick on Denny's hot cock. Denny struggled for composure as Merritt sucked him. Denny couldn't think straight. All he wanted was Merritt's mouth. And the rope-ties that kept him bound. Merritt pulled again, and the tension in Denny's arms intensified. Denny felt the roaring pulse of his orgasm tear through his body. Heat rose between them, Merritt sucking on Denny once more. When Denny got too close to coming, he came off his cock and, using Denny's juices, readied Denny's ass.

All Denny could do was move around, trying to get Merritt's sweet cock inside him, muttering, "Please, please." Denny thought he was losing his mind because Merritt was taking so long to move between Denny's legs.

"I tied you too well. You're so tight," Merritt said, trying to work his way into Denny.

"Do it! Fuck me. Now!"

And Merritt did.

Denny loved the heft of Merritt's body on top of his. Denny's entire being rejoiced at the fucking he took from Merritt. They rocked and bucked, Denny unable to hold Merritt in his arms, but they came hard and fast. Merritt buried deep inside Denny, the rope falling slack in his hand. The knot at Denny's groin produced wave after wave of pleasure as his trapped cock erupted between their trembling bodies.

Merritt whispered Denny's name and collapsed on top of him. He let out a loud groan. "And to think, this will only get better with time." Merritt unwound the ropes as lovingly as he'd tied them.

At long last, Denny was able to reach for Merritt, holding him in his arms as Denny's lavender water scented the darkening night air. They dozed on and off, drinking in every moment together that they could, Denny wishing this night would last forever.

114

Chapter Eight

Gremma knew how to dish out horrible spells and crippling hexes, but sure didn't know how to take one. She cried like a child as Merritt removed the cloak from her house. He was stunned to see teeth, hair, a child's tooth... so many very personal items sewn into it.

"Unpick each and every object in it, and hand them to me," Merritt instructed.

She did as he'd commanded, and, one by one, her warts evaporated.

"I never meant to hurt all those people," Gremma said. "Fortunata bewitched me. I feel so ashamed."

"You know why she banished you from the palace all those years ago, don't you?" he asked.

"Because I practiced spells on you and the household staff."

"Because you were more powerful than she, and Fortunata couldn't stand it."

This seemed to surprise her. "But—"

"She sought you out to help her in her evil deeds. Probably promised you would be welcomed back to the soft bosom of our family."

Her cheeks reddened. "Er. Ah. Something like that."

He reached into his pocket and produced the black candle. "This candle, once it has burned down, will kill you."

Gremma stared at him. "Why? How?"

"I know my sister told you that it had horse blood on it. Cillian's blood, to be precise."

Gremma's gaze shifted from left to right. *She's mortified. She can no longer look me in the eye.*

"But you made a grave error. She didn't cut Cillian and make a spell to harm me. She did it to kill you."

"That's ridiculous. I've done everything she's asked."

"Yes. And the ultimate test was that you had no idea what Cillian was."

She scrunched her nose. "A horse, wasn't he?"

"Yes, and no."

"What's that supposed to mean?"

"He was a descendent of the horse goddess, Epona."

Gremma gasped. "And I killed him?" She blinked continuously as she tried to absorb this.

"I can help you atone for this, but you must listen to me and follow my instructions to the letter."

Gremma cried, burying her face in her hands. "How could I not have known he was a special horse?"

Merritt grabbed her hands. "My sister cursed you. Controlled you. She took all your powers, as she did mine. She allowed you enough magic to help her with her spells but you couldn't even see that she had hexed the land around you. I realize now that Cillian died after eating the grass outside your house."

"My God. She's ruined me!" Gremma cried.

Merritt tried to calm her. "I can help, I promise you, but we don't have much time. Are you ready to be stronger than you've ever been in your life?"

She looked at him, and in that moment she seemed to pull herself together. "Yes. Yes, I can do this."

He grabbed her hand and the cloak, and they ran outside as rain fell so hard it seemed the very sky was about to collapse. God. Fortunata was angry.

So was Merritt. They came to the spot where Cillian had died but the horse was gone. Merritt put his fingers to his lips and whistled. From a distance, Merritt detected the soft whinnying answering his call, followed by the uncertain clomp of hooves.

"Quick," Merritt muttered and dragged Gremma through the rain.

"Merritt!" a female voice shouted. *Fortunata.*

In the distance, the shaky form of Cillian hovered into view. Merritt was so pleased to see the horse and to know he'd been able to undo Fortunata's vile magic that, at first, all he could do was touch the magnificent creature. Cillian put his head on Merritt's shoulder. Merritt received the message loud and clear.

"Come on!" he shouted to Gremma. "Get on his back. He'll take you where you need to go, then tell him to meet me in the ha-ha." He hoisted Gremma astride the horse. Most of her warts were gone and only half her hands were gnarled.

"You trust me?" She seemed stunned.

"No. But I trust him. One wrong move, Gremma, and I'll kill you myself."

Cillian turned gentle, trusting eyes on Merritt but walked away with Gremma clinging to his back. He would get stronger the longer they walked and the farther they got away from this place. Merritt closed his eyes and tried to locate his sister. All he saw was a wall of darkness.

Good.

For once, he'd blocked her and she couldn't read him. It didn't matter that it meant he couldn't read her. He had places to go and a certain pirate's court case to attend. He took the cloak that Gremma had woven and threw it over his shoulders. He would destroy it before he reached the court. Then, finally, the wretchedness Fortunata had wrought would be stopped.

Once and for all.

* * * *

Prison cell, Soriano Island...

The cell door jangled, and Denny opened an eye, unwilling to leave his beautiful dreamship. His hand was down his pants, so he quickly removed it. He glanced over his shoulder, surprised to see two Unseelie fairies there.

117

"Court is back in session," they tittered in unison.

He'd expected to re-enter the courtroom with Ebba and Barthelmass. He hoisted himself off the bed, nervous again. The dream had seemed so real it was painful to have to leave it. He'd returned to his ship after that sensational adventure with Merritt only to find Fortunata waiting for him.

"My brother's back in the sickbay. I fear he overdid it today."

Stricken with guilt, Denny hadn't been able to stop blaming himself. But Fortunta had seemed in buoyant spirits.

"I should check on him," Denny had said.

"You should eat the wonderful meal I prepared for you," she'd responded. She had made him a lavish dinner, plying him with rich red local wine and baked chicken with vegetables, the likes of which he'd never tasted.

Then, she'd attempted to seduce Denny, who'd rejected her. It had been horrible. He'd sprouted fairy wings and total panic in equal measure. Day and night, the dreadful scene played over and over in his head. Brother and sister had left the ship without Denny seeing or speaking to either again. All these months later, he had no idea how Merritt felt, or if Merritt missed him, too.

Now he was facing the courtroom again, that horrible place that would probably make him talk about what happened with Fortunata. With each new thing Ebba read aloud, it felt as though she was tossing knives into Denny's heart. His thoughts flew to Polly. He'd dreamed of his long search for her. Being incarcerated, he feared he was missing out on updates on her whereabouts. He'd wanted to head to Australia himself and had put away enough money to make such a trip. Now it seemed as though it had all been for naught.

Denny felt stricken by his helplessness. He could never have predicted that hearing details about his mother could hurt so much. The court would pick apart every aspect of his life. He screwed his eyes shut. He couldn't stand thinking about the things they said about his mother. Ebba knew more about her than he did. He'd had no idea she'd written to his dad, who had never mentioned it, but then Denny and his dad never spoke anymore. His life sounded worse when related by other people.

He allowed the fairies to fly him back to the courtroom and half hoped they'd drop him in the moat, but they didn't. They were strong and tough little blighters and managed to get him safely to the witness box. Once again, the bars snapped into place, the box rose, and, feeling like a caged animal, Denny took a moment to scan the courtroom.

His heart gave a lurch. A man dressed in an unusual kind of cape with a hood covering most of his face sat in the far left corner high against the roof. Denny could keep looking up during the trial and watch him. The man in the habit didn't move. Denny couldn't see his face but he knew it was him.

Am I ever going to see or touch that sweet face again? he wondered, his soul feeling like it might tear in two.

Since everybody else was busy gossiping, he sat in his seat observing the crowd as they, too, once again, took their places. The jury came in, led by the twin seers. The elderly black man with the telescope followed them. He stood right in front of Denny and stared at him through the spyglass. He lowered it for a moment, and Denny was surprised to see that the juror's eye had been sewn shut. There was no eye. The flesh around it had been slashed and scarred, but it was through this patch of skin that he studied Denny.

He bowed at Denny, who bent his head in acknowledgment, then scurried off to his seat. Denny wondered how the old man had managed to receive such a savage injury and, considering his advanced years, wondered if the man had dueled at dawn. His face appeared to have been cut by a sword.

The tall, thin, darkly dressed man with the necklace of human teeth came next, then a young African-looking woman in traditional garb. Denny recognized the textiles of her voluminous outfit as being Akwete cloth from the Igboland province in Nigeria. The fabric was made of hemp, which had intrigued Denny when he'd first transported the raw material to the Caribbean. It had interested him because of his early workhouse employment. There seemed to be constant reminders of it here.

He gazed at the woman, fascinated by her animated chatter with one of the twin seers. He had learned that the material was often used for masquerades and head gear for tribal warriors. The thought kept tumbling in his mind. *Masquerade.* Is she masquerading now? There was a middle-aged man who reminded Denny of a rooster with his cock's comb-like red hair, but the person who most delighted him was the elderly woman dressed in bright pink, purple and lime-green. Her hair was a glorious shade of fuchsia. He couldn't stop staring at it.

She had a raucous laugh when court wasn't in official action and slapped her knee constantly, rocking back and forth with mirth at anything anyone said to her, even when it didn't seem to be funny. Denny loved her hair. He'd always wished he'd had a grandma, a loving, kind lady who would tuck him into a soft, warm bed and make him cocoa. This lady seemed just the type to do that. He bet she made a good porridge too.

But his family wasn't like that. They weren't warm, touchy-feely types. His mother lacked the maternal gene, his father preferred his 'other woman' and Denny had never met any of his grandparents.

"Be lucky," his mother had said to him one time. "You would hate them. Your pa and I do. Royally!"

The jurors seemed animated and quirky in their own ways. He made up little histories for them in his mind. *I really should write, I have such a fertile imagination.* He looked around for Ebba and Barthelmass. They were standing in the middle of the courtroom and seemed to be in the middle of a heated discussion. That was not encouraging.

Suddenly, Pegasus snorted and pawed at the ground. Everybody stopped talking and rushed to their seats. After everybody had settled, the judge restored order in the courtroom with his gavel. Ebba stood and asked her first question of Denny.

"We haven't yet discussed your mutiny. Is it true Captain Lester Piggins was a cruel man?"

"He was. And I daresay he still is. I believe he's endured no less than three mutinies."

"What is it about him that's so terrible?"

"He rapes, plunders, pillages, all while pretending to be an honorable man." Denny paused. Thinking of Piggins made his blood boil. "He let me and several of my senior officers languish in a prison in Tarragona. I later found out he was involved in a high-stakes game of mountebank, a Spanish card game. Piggins had perfected a kind of scam of the game and wanted to keep in the good graces of the jailers so he left us there."

"And what happened there?"

"I was sexually abused. It was known to Piggins, but still he allowed it to continue."

The twin seers shook their heads in unison. Denny kept his wits about him. Yes, he'd learned much at Christoph's hand, but the fact remained, Piggins had known that Denny was being taken daily to Christoph's office but had done nothing to help.

Denny tried not to dwell on the subject and found it hard to look people in the eye.

Ebba cleared her throat, making Denny catch her attention. "When you staged your mutiny, what did you do to Piggins?"

Denny looked at her. "He had swindled some sailors in a game of mountebank in the same sea port where he'd let his crew suffer. These were young lads who could ill afford to lose their wages. I took command of the crew and the ship when Piggins refused to return the money he'd falsely won. I handed him over to the authorities there."

A handful of courtroom watchers burst into applause until the judge banged his gavel. "Enough!" he cried.

"And as far as you know, he's no longer in prison and has moved on to captain other ships," Ebba said.

"Yes."

"We talked earlier of your many rescues of slaves. Would you say the portions of oceans known as the Triangular Transatlantic Slave Trade is a popular target for pirates such as yourself?"

Where is she going with this? "I guess so," he said, warily.

She gave him an odd look he interpreted as 'Go on'.

So he did. "Cargo ships traveling from Europe to the African coast, as an example, would trade manufactured goods and weapons for slaves. The traders would then sail to the Caribbean to sell the slaves. They would return to Europe with sugar, tobacco and cocoa. Some of the ships heading to Europe would carry raw materials such as different metals, stone and wood, in exchange for things like manufactured goods, preserved cod and rum. Some of these would then be taken to the Caribbean, where they were exchanged for sugar and molasses."

"So it is a profitable business."

"Yes. A hard business. Some ships struggle with storm damage and food shortage, but yes, it's a profitable line of work."

"And your ship, the La-Di-Da, made money?"

"Well, yes. Ships that traded in the Triangular Transatlantic Slave Trade were able to make money at each stop."

"And being a pirate ship, you were able to make money this way, too?"

"Yes. We didn't hoist the pirate flag when we pulled into port. Only on the high seas."

Ebba nodded. "That's why you were able to get away with piracy for so long."

He thought for a moment. "Yes. We'd also switched routes. A lot of piracy had left the North Atlantic Ocean—"

"Why?"

122

"They are notoriously tough waters. Bad storms that sometimes last for days. We were all experienced seamen and took advantage of the dwindling pirate trade."

"So even though you were making money, you still saw fit to attack other vessels and kill the people on board?"

Some of the courtroom watchers gasped. Denny flicked a gaze up to the hooded man who twitched in his seat.

"That's what pirates do," Denny said, "though I took pride in not killing men. I have personally killed less than ten."

"But didn't you have a crewmember you rescued from a ship that sank in Honduras who went mad and shot seventeen people at sea?"

Another collective gasp.

"That never happened under my command. That was before we staged our mutiny. Our captain was a cruel man, a drunk. He took on a rigger who said he needed work. I'd heard he was part of a gang that had stolen a sloop and had pirated all over the islands, but the captain wouldn't listen to me. The first ship we encountered, Jackson Garfield— that was the rigger's name—he grabbed some guns and started shooting. We were able to restrain him, and when we landed in Honduras, he was forced to leave the ship. We learned his gang had pirated another ship and had stolen a container of logs that had been destined for Boston."

"So these were bad men."

"Yes."

"But you didn't kill any of them."

Denny smiled. "No."

"But you killed a very good man. An Italian explorer you and your pirate crew picked up in Seville."

Denny hated her in that moment, more than he had ever hated another living being. He breathed deeply, ready to scream with the pain and unfairness of having to kill such a wonderful man. He fought tears and looked down at his hands. In that moment, he understood where she was going. This was one of his worst memories. It had destroyed him to take the life of Giovanni Ricci. It had been such an ordeal that he recalled every second of it and regretted the necessity to end his life to this very day.

"Yes," he said, his voice coming out a whisper. He blinked back tears. He'd always suspected he'd never get over what had happened, but now he knew for sure.

"Please tell the court the circumstances of this killing."

Denny sighed. "Our ship stopped in Seville and we discovered a few crewmembers from an Italian ship that had been damaged in a storm. The Rigoletta was in such poor condition, it required months of strenuous repair. The Italian explorer, Giovanni Ricci, who had led the expedition had sailed far off course and told me that his crew had sickened during their voyage. Some had died. He wanted to return to Bilbao, another town in Spain, where two of his remaining crewmembers had been taken in by monks who were caring for them. He was worried about them. I gladly took him and the three crewmen accompanying him. He was enamored of canned food, as many seamen are—"

"Why is that?" Ebba asked.

"One gets sick of rancid meat that is salted to preserve it. With canned food, you can enjoy things like New York oysters, or French sardines canned right there in the beautiful port of Nantes. Nothing is more delicious than canned Italian fruit." He grinned at the memory of his first bite of canned peaches. "Pennsylvania tomatoes are other foods we seamen adore."

"So what happened?" Ebba drew him away from his reverie. Unfortunately.

"Signore Ricci was trying to be as unobtrusive as possible. He didn't want special meals cooked for him, though I became aware very quickly that he was quite ill. His crewmembers seemed to be starving and fell upon the food we gave them. Signore Ricci refused to be a burden. He had a few remaining cans of food and ate one. Have you ever seen lead poisoning?"

"No," Ebba said. "I have not."

124

"I have," the twin seers said in unison, raising their hands. Every head in the courtroom turned in their direction.

"'Tis a cruel death," they said as one.

Denny became choked up and struggled to continue. "This poor man had no idea that he was making himself sick. When he opened one of the cans, my cook realized it smelled bad. The food was gray in color, but Signore Ricci insisted on eating it. He had no clue that the contents were poisoned with lead because of cheap manufacturing. He became extremely ill on board. He fell into delirium. We could not get him to Bilbao fast enough."

The twin seers held their hands to their mouths, as though they could see the awful images swimming in Denny's mind.

"He became unable to walk or breathe. He was given to violent episodes of vomiting and it was heartbreaking to watch. His bones and every muscle in his body caused him agony. His skin turned a very strange color. He was ashen, as though he'd been lit by fire from within."

"Exactly," the seers said once again in unison. They nodded.

Denny felt a stab of gratitude for their acknowledgment. He *had* made the right decision.

"Signore Ricci's crewmembers had suspected the food was contaminated and had refused to eat it for weeks. They had been starving. Poor Signore Ricci poisoned himself badly and it was clear he was suffering and would not survive the sea journey. Please understand I did not want to kill him. He begged me to do it."

Denny dropped his head and recalled the awful moment when he'd complied. "It was the hardest thing I have ever had to do and I am not a sentimental man. He was a good, kind man who could no longer tolerate the pain. He vomited black bile and could barely speak at the end. It took every bit of remaining strength for him to beg me, to convince me to end his agony." He was silent for a long time, remembering.

"How did you do it?" Ebba asked, her tone hushed.

"I shot him. We wrapped him in cloth and gave him to the monks when we reached dry land in Bilbao. His body had the stench of lead poisoning. I've never experienced it before. It is a metallic smell. The monks instructed us to wash ourselves thoroughly when we arrived. None of Signore Ricci's other crewmembers survived, except for the two we had on board. The ones he'd left in Bilbao had also passed. I learned from the two men that had traveled with us on my ship that Signore Ricci had fed his crew well until sickness hit them. He often went hungry to make sure they ate. He had assumed that rancid meat was the cause of their illness, ignoring his crewmen's suggestions that it was the canned goods. His death was not something I took lightly."

"Thank you," Ebba said. "Was there ever an occasion where you killed a good man in different circumstances?"

"In an act of self-protection, yes. Twice. Other times, I killed pirates and slave traders. I don't regret those. They were not good men."

"What about Carter Henning?"

Denny stared at her in surprise. *How does she know about him?* "He was a pirate."

"You didn't know it at the time, did you?"

Denny grew restless. Ebba had been on the ship at that time and knew exactly what had happened.

"He was a bad man," he said, staring her right in the eyes.

"You took over his sloop, didn't you?"

"I knew him before that." He could tell that shocked her. "I'd met him a few years ago on another sloop, briefly. I didn't trust him then. He tried to sell me torn fabric, keeping the damaged portions rolled up, but I checked them and refused to complete the purchase."

Ebba was so thrown it seemed that she paused to turn pages in her notebook. Denny couldn't figure out her strategy. One moment she seemed to be on his side, the next she appeared to be trying to hang him. He glanced up, and the man in the caped hood raised a hand. His thumb pointed up. That was when Denny realized Ebba was trying to lull Denny into a false sense of confidence. She was building up to something big. She thought she had something on him that she couldn't. Denny was the first to admit he had secrets, but nothing he thought would be of value to a court. He hoped.

He waited in silence while she consulted her notes. He kept a clear head. He had to be careful of his thoughts. Especially with this sharp jury.

"I think we've heard enough for tonight," the judge ordered. "We'll finish for the evening and daybreak isn't far away. Some of our participants have dawn curfews thanks to their particular curses." He banged his gavel. "Court will reconvene at nine o'clock tomorrow morning."

Chapter Nine

Merritt watched everything and wished he could join Denny. He wished he could take him and drag him to the nearest ship away from here.

Soon, he promised himself. The crowd got up en masse and surged toward the doors. Fairy guards escorted Denny to the cells. Merritt remained in his seat. It took him a long time to leave the courtroom. He knew Denny had seen him, and for one moment, Merritt worried that everybody present had been able to see the sparks flying between them. Merritt gripped the low marble wall of the balcony and closed his eyes. All that Denny had been through was worse than Merritt had imagined.

When at last he left the court, he knew it was time to get rid of the cloak. He slipped out of the building and, making sure nobody followed him, he made his way to the small, ancient church opposite the modern and massive court house. Centuries ago, Merritt and Fortunata's parents had fled their own island kingdom in England and traveled here, establishing a new and happy kingdom. They'd embraced and welcomed all in the magical world, eventually being betrayed and murdered by people they'd trusted.

Everything had changed when they'd allowed outsiders — Western sea traders and ships containing sick men aboard that no magic could cure. His thoughts flew to Denny and the Italian explorer he'd been forced to kill.

Merritt and Fortunata had grown up without their parents, trusting only each other. Fortunata had such a wonderful, glorious side to her, but constant loss and romantic failure had clouded her judgment. She had never been a happy girl, in spite of having everything. Having so much power and weaving chaotic spells didn't seem to bring her joy, or peace of mind. In fact, she had become dangerously delusional. It had begun on the ship when they'd been abducted. She hadn't been able to protect herself. Or Merritt. Instead of being grateful that Merritt had found love, she'd tried her hardest to disparage and discredit Denny, even though he'd saved them.

Inside the church, Merritt lifted off the hood and removed the cloak. The memories and bad feelings his sister and cousin had woven into it would find peace in this beautiful place. He was the only one in his family who came here. A soft whinny told him that Cillian had arrived. Merritt opened the backdoor, and the horse, standing on the small grassy knoll they'd called the ha-ha as children, came down the slope and trotted inside.

Merritt laughed. The priest would have a fit if he saw the horse in his church, but Merritt let Cillian sniff and paw his way around the apse. Seeming antsy, Cillian moved to the ambulatory on either side of the apse, then he spun around and, tail swishing, made his way past the pews normally reserved for the choir to the transept, almost in the middle of the building. When he stopped and clomped a hoof in a certain section, Merritt knew this was the spot.

"Back to the palace, Cillian," he said. "Go, my friend. Find Avery. I will see you very soon."

Cillian shook his great head. He didn't want to leave him.

Merritt stroked the horse's mane and flank. "We've been together so long, I promise, this isn't goodbye."

Cillian's bright, warm eyes bore into his.

"I will be home soon," Merritt whispered, wrapping his arms around the great stallion's neck.

At last, Cillian left, Merritt glad that he would return to Avery, who would rub him down and feed him well. As long as he'd known Cillian, this was the only time Merritt was aware of him ever dying. Thank God he'd returned. Good had triumphed over evil.

Merritt waited until the sky grew dark. He knew the priest who served here would be with the jurors discussing the case. The judge's sudden command to cut the proceedings short worried Merritt. He had to move fast. Once he was certain he was alone, he dug into the hardened earth blocks in the ground with a ceremonial dagger from the altar table. Beneath the stone lay his parents' ashes in sealed caskets. Merritt had never actually seen them before and became emotional when he found them covered in dust, but intact.

Their parents' enemies must never know where their ashes were. Even a small amount could give their enemies power. Only a few people knew their precise location. The priest, Cillian, and now Merritt. He folded the cloak and stuffed it into the small space. Beside it, he lay the small gold cross belonging to the priest. Merritt had found it on the altar in Gremma's house. He had no idea what Fortunata intended to do with it, but she hadn't begun her magic on it. Now she never would. In the encroaching darkness, he replaced the stone block and filled in the dirt. He cleaned off the ceremonial dagger he'd used, hoping God wouldn't mind his using it, then, when he was certain all trace of his work was gone, he left the church.

Merritt visited the four remaining owners of the hexed items and returned their belongings to them. By the time he returned to the palace, he'd had a long and exhausting day and he wanted nothing more than a hot bath, some food then sleep. He stopped by the stables first and found Cillian covered in a blanket and eating hay.

"He seems somehow different," Avery remarked, rubbing Cillian's nose.

"How so?"

"A little younger."

Merritt didn't say anything for a moment, then he asked, "Did he have a wound when he came back this morning?"

"Aye." Avery looked surprised. "I was able to fix it, but I still have no idea how he managed to hurt himself."

"It was my sister," Merritt whispered. "I want you to

leave the palace with him. He's not safe here."

"But—"

Merritt pressed a bag of gold into Avery's hands. "I will get you more. But until you hear from me, you are to keep him in the stables by the forge."

"Smitty's forge?"

Merritt nodded. "If anyone asks, I'll say Cillian needs new shoes."

"He does need new shoes, but I thought Smitty was under the weather."

"Smitty's in fine fettle now." Merritt grabbed Avery's arms and looked into his eyes. "Neither of you are to come back here until you hear from me directly. Don't believe any messages. Don't listen to anybody. I will come to you myself."

"Yes, sir," Avery said. "Are we to leave right now?"

Merritt nodded. "Yes. Just wait until I get my sister out of the way." Merritt raced outside and caught Fortunata creeping toward the stables.

"Hello, sis," he said, hands on hips.

Fortunata gave a soft little shriek. "You scared me."

Good. "We need to talk."

"About what?" she asked, looking evasive. Even in the near darkness, her sudden fear was palpable.

"I've destroyed the spells you cast. I've taken off all the hexes. How could you do this to the people we know and love?"

"I never—"

"Don't lie. I know everything."

A myriad emotions crossed her face. "What have you done with Gremma?"

"Sent her someplace safe."

She let out a sigh. "And the cloak?"

"Gone." He paused. "Can you explain yourself?"

Fortunata looked emotional when she said, "I know this will sound weird, but I did it out of love."

"Love?" he scoffed. "You don't know the meaning of the

131

word."

"Yes, I do. I love you and I am so afraid you'll leave me. I thought...I thought if I kept you sedated, sort of here and not here, you wouldn't miss him." She shook her head. "But you still love him. And I know he loves you. I have never had anyone who loves me like that. Never."

"Perhaps if you didn't try hexing your lovers you might fare better."

"What are you talking about?"

"The love spells, Fortunata. You can't help yourself. Like all of your spells, they backfire."

"They don't backfire. They just don't always go the way I want them to." She blew out a sigh. "I'm sorry. I'm especially sorry about the horse. I know how much you love him. Sometimes I think you love him more than me."

"I do, as it happens."

She gasped.

"Cillian never grated his fingernails into my coffee in order to keep my loyalty. He never drugged me or kept me a prisoner in my room. I know you think you love me, but you don't know the meaning, and now, I need a hot bath and a lot of space from you."

"But—"

"Not now, Fortunata." He held up a hand. "Just give me time." He stalked away, surprised when two men from Denny's old pirate ship approached him.

"It's Rigby, isn't it?" Merritt asked.

"Aye, sir, glad you remember me." Rigby looked shifty-eyed when he said, "Cap'n Denny managed to escape. He gave me a note to give you. Hopes you can meet him."

Rigby handed him the note. Merritt took it just as Fortunata came up behind him.

"What's going on here?" she asked.

Rigby and his friend took off.

"He brought me a note from Denny."

"Impossible," Fortunata said. "Sweetie, it's a trap."

"And I'm to believe you? The worst liar of all?"

132

"I promise you, Denny is in his prison cell. He cannot escape."

"How can I trust you? You've kept us apart all these months."

"I'm sorry. Truly, I am sorry, but I don't believe Rigby. I cannot believe Denny sent that note."

"Well," Merritt said, mustering up more confidence than he actually felt, "that's a chance I am going to have to take."

Merritt opened the note but in the blanketing darkness couldn't read much. He picked out the words 'ship' and 'harbor' and ran toward the ocean. His breath caught in his throat. His lost love! He couldn't wait to see Denny and ignored Fortunata, who screamed his name.

"It's a trap!" she yelled at the same moment Rigby jumped in front of him.

Rigby threw a punch, which Merritt easily ducked. Rigby threw another punch, which glanced off Merritt's chin. Dazed, Merritt swung back, aiming for Rigby's solar plexus. He hit him, surprising Rigby who reeled back, letting out a loud, "Oof."

Somebody came up from behind Merritt. He turned to see Fortunata attempting to fight off the man Merritt had seen earlier with Rigby.

"No!" she yelled, laying her ineffective fists on him.

Rigby came roaring back and attacked Merritt once more.

"Do something!" Merritt yelled at Fortunata. Of all the times for her to suddenly stop throwing spells.

Rigby took Merritt to the ground, another sailor racing over to help him. Merritt fought them both.

"He has courage!" Rigby yelled with a laugh. "The pirate's whore can fight!"

Merritt flew into a rage. "Help me!" he shouted at Fortunata whose face was a blur as Merritt tumbled on the ground with the two pirates.

"You weren't supposed to hurt him," she shrieked at Rigby. "Somebody's coming! Take him. Now!" She waved her hand at Merritt, who sank into nothingness. The whole world turned black.

* * * *

Denny had lost all track of time but was exhausted. He knew he would sleep as soon as he lay on his bed.

He couldn't think straight, let alone have a serious conversation with Ebba, who chattered at him nonstop all the way back to his cell. He wished she would go away. She went on and on about her fears that the jury would dislike him because of his rough edges and his hard life.

"I've done my best," he said. "But it's not over yet, right?"

"Maybe not." She looked flustered. "Usually when the jury calls for a session to end early they've already reached a verdict and they leave it in the judge's hands. They will give you an opportunity to accept their offer."

"You mean the trial is possibly over?"

"Maybe. We can discuss it if and when the offer is made but I am pretty certain they will make an offer before we go to court in the morning."

"What do you think they'll offer?" he asked, using the last remnants of water in his cell's drinking glass to clean his teeth.

Ebba seemed to find something of tremendous interest in his barren wall space.

"What?" he asked.

She did an odd thing. She pressed her hand against the beige-colored wall and pushed, as though expecting a secret door to emerge. "I don't think you will receive the death sentence."

"That's a relief."

She swallowed. "I suspect they will offer you life imprisonment, or a lifetime of slavery."

"Such exciting choices."

She looked at him. "Which are you most inclined to accept?"

"I have no idea," he said, wondering if she had already

been given an offer to present to him. She would just have to wait. He was more convinced than ever that she had no intention of helping him, but didn't want to see him hang, either.

"How is your brother?" he asked.

"Fair. He's in the infirmary. They gave him a draught. He enjoys those. They help him sleep."

Denny didn't respond. He hated medicine and couldn't remember the last time he'd had a draught. He recalled now he'd taken one years ago for a tooth extraction. It hadn't done much to ease the terrible pain. The memory came back so vividly he could feel the tooth aching all over again.

He lay on his bed facing away from her. He was tired of all this. Maybe execution would be a release.

"I'll be back tomorrow," she said, giving him a comforting pat on the back. The truth was he'd always seen himself as invincible. Perhaps most men did. He'd never thought that he would end up on trial for his life. For a long time, he lay on his side staring at the wall. Perhaps it was apt. It was blank, like his future. He had to face facts. It was unlikely he'd be a free man again. His life as he'd known it was over.

Gone.

Given the choice of imprisonment, or a lifetime of slavery, he'd have to consider which option would best give him the means for crafting an escape. He had his wings, didn't he? He could fly. How far or for how long, he had no idea. He suspected the slavery option involved having one of his wings clipped, just like the cursed pirate eagle, Howard deGacy.

Denny kept pondering his problem. Upon his intake, everybody had made a big deal about his inability to fly, and his painful wings. He was starting to hurt now and needed more nectar. *Maybe I will die in my sleep. That would end all my problems.* He closed his eyes, the mess that had become his life parading around in his mind like a French carousel. *Stop the world. I want to get off.*

135

Utter desolation consumed him. He blinked back hot tears. *I'm a fairy. No, I mean, I'm a pirate. Pirates don't cry!*

He tried to will himself back to his favorite daydream, his one and only deeply erotic encounter with Merritt, but his mind wouldn't cooperate. The cell door lock jangled, and half expecting the tittering of Unseelie fairies, he was surprised to see the door swinging open but nobody there. A sudden chill descended on the room like a thick, wet blanket as he tried to sit up on his bed. Cold tendrils of pain shot out around him, pinning him to the mattress. Thick, wet tentacles wrapped him in their invisible embrace. Stunned, he tried to breathe, but it was like being smothered by a big, slobbering, unseen octopus. Whatever it was that held him sucked at his face, chest and arms. He was powerless to fight it. The thing pressed on Denny's heart as though trying to work its way inside his body. Denny tried to fend off the harrowing attack but couldn't move.

They sentenced me to death. And this is how I am going to die.

His mind kept spinning. Bones snapped in his torso and the screams coming out of his own mouth frightened him. The thing crushed Denny's wings, then invaded his mouth. Denny gave in then when his heartbeat hammered in his head. He saw Merritt's face in his mind. And his sister's. He knew now that she hadn't gone on to some merry life in Australia. She was in trouble and he could no longer help. Just as he thought the end was coming, the thing backed away from him.

Something puffed in his face. "Huh-huh." An unusual smell like sausages invaded the small space.

"Is he still alive?" a soft voice whispered. Was it a woman?

"Enough, Cetus," a harsh masculine voice responded.

Cetus? Denny opened his mouth to scream but no sound emerged. He'd heard tales of this infamous sea monster that was part octopus, part human and dragon too. Other seamen had warned him that the creature lurked in the ocean surrounding the Caribbean. He would have dismissed the stories as the result of too much liquor on the high seas, but the people who'd reported to him had seemed terrified months after their encounter with this Cetus creature. After he'd been cursed, Denny had learned first-hand that anything was possible.

He finally managed to sit on his bed, wondering if Cetus would lunge at him again. Denny's whole body shook as he struggled to regain his breath. It took every ounce of effort in him to do so. A fresh wave of pain tore through him and, suddenly, his feet were wet. He glanced down, his mouth opening wider into a silent scream. The floor to the cell was receding and his bed disappeared into the wall behind him. He was in a cave. An ice blue, watery cave with slippery steps that appeared to have people's faces frozen beneath them.

A strange roar invaded the space, and Denny finally looked up and his heart almost gave up its fight. He'd never seen anything like the strange, floating sea-green blob with bones protruding from its head and back. Angry red eyes stared at him from a mountain of wavering, spiky tentacles that seemed to make up his hair and face.

His hands were webbed with sharp talons that Denny knew the creature was dying to use. Blood dripped from them, and Denny's voice came out in a frightened squeak. He looked down at his chest and saw that he'd been ripped and slashed. Denny fell down the sharp, icy steps to land on the bottom of the cave floor.

"My clothes," he whispered. He was naked and his wings felt as though they were on fire as he lay on his side, trying to catch his breath. He was afraid, and also unable to move his arms to feel them. He swallowed as the monster came toward him once more.

"Cetus. Stop!" the female voice shrieked.

From somewhere ice cracked and frigid water dripped onto Denny's head and back. The agony it caused was indescribable. His skin was white. He knew he was freezing to death.

"Put his clothes back on," the woman insisted. Denny

knew that voice. "We haven't condemned him... Yet."

Denny looked around him but couldn't tell where the female voice was coming from since it was just him and Mr. Ugly in the cave room. Denny kept shivering, the condensation from his breath coming out in thick puffs as he gave his full attention to just trying to breathe.

"Cetus!" the female voice commanded.

The sea creature roared, opening his mouth to reveal row after row of tiny shark heads, all screaming and snapping their jaws. Denny tried turning his head away, but was still unable to move so he closed his eyes, uttering a silent prayer: *I am sorry, God. I really am.* He couldn't bear to see those hideous jaws coming for him. The cold, meaty breath swamped him as Cetus advanced on him, then suddenly a crack of thunder reverberated in the room and the sea monster squealed and retreated, one huge, webbed claw hugging the cave floor, the other pointing at Denny. The creature was furious.

"Back, Cetus. *Now.*"

The creature whined as he scurried back and disappeared into a spray of ocean water.

Silence.

For several minutes, Denny waited. The cave warmed and from nowhere his clothes appeared on his body. They seemed covered in beige slime. The sea monster. Denny wanted to be sick but footsteps in the distances made him stop and listen. They were coming from the far left. He was surprised when the monk's habit appeared and whoever wore it moved quickly toward him.

"Merritt?" Denny's voice came out in a whisper. The hood on the habit fell back and Denny almost screamed. "Fortunata." He had nowhere to run, nowhere to move. He'd known she'd been around but from the moment he'd landed here, nobody had spoken of her without trepidation. Like Denny, they all seemed afraid of her. He tried not to show his fear, but she skewered him with a look.

"My brother came to watch your trial and he was abducted

late last night," she said. She was as beautiful as ever but grief had etched hard lines around her eyes and red rims that, even now, threatened to spill over with tears.

"Abducted?" He squinted at her. "Surely you can't think I had anything to do with it."

"No. I know you are not responsible."

"Then why...all this?" He shrugged, looking around the cave. "Have you heard anything? Is Merritt in good health?"

She looked at him a moment. "The trial had a hung jury. Two of the jurors feel you can never heal from the things that have happened to you and that you can never be a good man."

"Which two were they?"

"The twin seers," she said.

That shocked him. He didn't know how to respond. "I thought they liked me," he whined when he'd recovered from the news.

"They do, which is why they have agreed to change their vote."

"Really? What did you all decide?" Denny held his breath with anticipation.

"The others feel you deserve a second chance. So the seers have a question. They sense you have aspects of goodness. I am willing to give you the opportunity to prove it."

"You said they have a question?"

"Yes. A question about love."

"Love?" What was she talking about?

The twin seers' voices emerged from somewhere deep in the cave. Denny couldn't see them but heard them clearly. "There is one thing you can do to persuade us to change our minds," they said in unison. "Prove you are worthy of being loved and trusted."

"How?" He couldn't help the sulky tone.

Fortunata spoke then. "Rescue my brother for me."

"I can but try." He paused. "Why do I feel there is the weight of many conditions on this?"

139

"Because you're not as stupid as you look."

"Thanks a lot."

"It's a compliment, you buffoon."

He was a prisoner of a lunatic woman in a horrible cave. He was in no position to argue.

"We know who took him. I am willing to let you rescue him because I know you have genuine feelings for my brother, and because his captors would never suspect you would be able to come for him."

"Who are his captors?"

She gazed at him, a malicious gleam to her eye as she said, "Pirate Captain Rigby."

Denny's eyes widened. "He's not a captain. He's a second mate!" Taking a moment to absorb the shock he asked, "Are you sure he took Merritt?"

"Oh yes. The fool is attempting a ransom. He sent Merritt a note, pretending it had come from you. Of course, Merritt fell into the trap and raced to meet you and got caught."

Denny became enraged. "He tricked him?" He wanted to kill Rigby right then and there.

"Trust me, when I get my hands on him, he won't just be sprouting fairy wings."

Denny looked at her. "He wouldn't hurt him again. He wouldn't put him in chains. He might be all kinds of a monster, but—"

"Oh no. He likes Merritt. He just wants a lot of money for his safe return."

Denny couldn't deny himself a stab of jealousy. "I didn't know Rigby was homosexual. Are they...ah... Are they lovers?"

"Of course not." She looked indignant. "My brother thinks he's in love with you."

Denny couldn't resist a smile.

She narrowed her eyes and shook her head. "Rigby's attraction to my brother is purely financial. Things haven't been good between me and Merritt since we left your ship."

Denny waited. There was nothing to say. She had to know

Denny, too, was miserable.

She sighed. "Somehow, Rigby has managed to obscure his exact location from my attempts to find him. If anyone can see through his web of spells, it's you."

"Web of spells? What do you mean?"

Fortunata looked to her right, and Denny noticed the twin seers emerging from the shadows.

"You're right. He really doesn't know."

"I don't know what?" Denny wanted to scratch his head but still couldn't move his hands.

"Rigby is a powerful sorcerer. He lied to me about you and made me think you were the sorcerer. I see I was wrong now."

"That's why you whammied me?" Denny stared at her.

"And you rejected me." She sniffed.

"I told you that you were beautiful. I also told you I don't fancy women. It was nothing personal."

She held up a hand, a pained expression on her face. "The two sisters here have helped me see the error of my ways." As though to ward off any argument or questions from Denny she said, "I am willing to offer you a handsome reward for my brother's recovery."

"Like what?" He had no idea why he was being so sullen but he didn't trust her one bit.

"You don't trust me." It was a statement, not a question.

"No, I don't. Look what you did to me."

She pulled a face. "I can't change it, and I'll confess I can practice no magic without my brother being here. We're bonded by an old family curse and our powers lie in each other's well-being."

He absorbed this a moment. "So when can I start looking for him?"

"Wait," she said. "This depends upon your answer..." She gestured to the twin seers, who looked at her, then at each other, then down at Denny, who was still on the cave floor.

Denny gulped. "I'm ready," he said, trying not to focus

on the fact that neither of the twins appeared to have feet and they looked even stranger up close and personal. They had bird-like features with eyes that blinked and took in everything. Their long blue robes had a musty smell. *Whatever question they have, I bet it's a doozy. I hope they don't ask me the meaning of life or love. What's the meaning of anything?*

"We want to know about your relationship with Merritt," the twins said in unison.

"Fire away." *Oops. Those are dangerous words around here.*

"What exactly are your feelings for him?" they asked.

"Oh, that's easy. I felt sure he understood me and I loved him for every aspect of what he did and who he loved. I had a complete...a resting place finally."

The twin seers stared at him. "And what is the meaning of life?" they asked him.

When he looked stumped they tittered, pointing at him. "Only joking," they said.

"There are a couple of things you need to understand if you are to take this mission," Fortunata said, holding up a hand to stop the tide of bird-like giggles. "One. You are to bring my brother home. If you want to be with him, you will need to live here."

"Here?" He peered around him.

"Not here, you buffoon."

"You're rather fond of that word, aren't you?"

"I think it's apt where you're concerned." She rolled her eyes. "I meant here on the island. You can live in the palace with us." Fortunata leaned down to him and enunciated carefully, "I cannot and will not live without my brother."

"Understood. I don't like living without him either." He took a deep breath. "You're inviting me to live in that big, sparkly palace with you and Merritt?"

"Yes."

"I don't believe you," he said.

"Well!"

"I've learned from experience that you're a switchy witch.

142

Why should I trust you?"

The twin seers turned in unison and stared at her. "You must tell him."

"Oh, all right." Fortunata glowered at them, then at Denny. "Once you return with him you can never leave the island. I have promised the judge I won't place anymore whammies on people of the high seas. I can't do that unless I never leave here. I have a terrible temper, you know."

"Really? I hadn't noticed."

The twin seers giggled. Fortunata glared at them.

"Is the rest of your island nicer than this?" Denny asked.

She gave him a sharp glance. "It's paradise. Well, most of it is. I'm going to clean up the port and stop all the trials. The judge and jury want to retire anyway."

He thought for a moment. That sounded pretty good to him but he missed his sister terribly. Could he live without being able to keep searching for Penny?

"I have one other thing that might persuade you to stay here," Fortunata said. "I have arranged for the rescue of your sister. I know where she is and I can bring her to you. And that is a promise."

Chapter Ten

Merritt was chained to a bed. Delirium held him.

"What did she do to him?" a male voice asked.

"She said it was a sleeping spell, but he's been unconscious for days. He keeps muttering, 'Denny'."

Denny.

Merritt smiled. Ah. He was having his favorite dream. Sometimes the dream hurt because when he awakened, Denny seemed farther away than ever. Right now, the dream seemed real, and helped him to want to live.

"I'm here, my love," Denny said, reaching for him. They were in the room, the only one they'd ever shared as lovers. "I'm here." Denny pressed him against the cool white wall, kissing him. Denny kept interrupting their heated embrace to stroke Merritt's cheek, as though he couldn't believe he was real. Somehow he was real. Merritt could taste and touch Denny's beautiful mouth. He needed more. So much more. Merritt pulled up Denny's shirt, fumbling with the buttons.

"Your wings are gone," Merritt murmured.

Denny's laughter filled the sunlit room. His shirt fell to the floor, his gaze one of soulful intent as he pulled Merritt to him and kissed him again. Merritt ran his hands all over Denny's body, exhilarating at the rippling muscles in his arms, chest and back. He moved down to Denny's pants where his rigid cock strained against the tight fabric.

Denny tore at Merritt's clothing, too, peeling off the layers as fast as he could. "Did you dress to torment me?" he asked. "I've never seen so many undergarments."

Merritt laughed as Denny bent and took down Merritt's pants, dropping succulent kisses on his neck and chest. He fell to his knees and moaned as he reached Merritt's cock. Denny let his tongue do the talking. He licked the shaft from base to tip then back again. Merritt's cock sprang into Denny's mouth, making both men moan. Denny drew his warm mouth over the length and sucked it in gently, picking up speed as their mingled cries filled the air. Merritt kept touching and holding Denny's head, stroking his bristled cheeks.

Denny leaned back on his haunches, his own cock pointing up toward Merritt.

Merritt leaned down and touched the tip but it wasn't enough. He lifted his foot and pushed Denny onto his back. Denny laughed, reaching up for him.

Voices invaded their passionate encounter but Merritt ignored them.

"Get on me," Denny rasped, pulling Merritt toward him. He flipped Merritt around so that Merritt knelt over Denny's face, his ass right above Denny's mouth.

Denny grabbed Merritt's hips and raised his head so that his tongue could reach Merritt's hole. He licked and sucked with abandon, the sounds inflaming Merritt's own needs. He lowered his head and sucked Denny's cock. It leaked as Merritt drew it into his mouth, the juices salty and sweet. Denny let out a moan which Merritt echoed. Denny lifted Merritt just a little so that he could capture Merritt's cock with lips and tongue.

The two men worked on each other, their sucking fast and dirty.

Merritt felt the wave of pleasure build inside him. He couldn't have stopped sucking Denny if his life depended on it. They came together, crashing hard. Tears filled Merritt's eyes as Denny wrapped his arms around him and came off his cock, whispering, "I'll never let you go."

* * * *

Denny choked on his emotions as he looked up at Fortunata. "How do you know where my sister is? Is she — ?"

"You love her the way I love my brother. She's in a very

145

bad place but I have two trusted men watching over her. I can, and will, bring her back here."

"Where is she? Please. I've been searching for her for so long."

Fortunata studied him for a moment. "She's in England."

"England! How did she wind up there?"

"She never left. You were lied to. Now. If you'll get to your feet, we'll get started."

Denny rose, not sure his legs would work. Polly was in England! No wonder he had been unable to track her in Australia. *All these years...* His list of enemies was growing.

"Don't dwell on things," Fortunata insisted as the twin seers produced a pair of leather boots and a sword and gun for him.

"These weapons are decoration only. They won't work until you're in open water," Fortunata told him. "So don't get any ideas about killing me or anybody else here and trying to escape."

"I won't," he lied. The truth was, though he was plenty mad at her for giving him a great big bloody pair of wings, he was useless. He couldn't even walk without wobbling. He lurched like a mad old drunk until one of the seers handed him a gold goblet. *Ah, nectar.* He drank it quickly, feeling much better. He shrugged, testing his wings. They only twinged a bit now. He and Fortunata left the cave by a hole the twin seers conjured in the wall. Denny would have been flabbergasted but he'd come to expect weirdness with this lot.

As he stepped outside, he breathed in the fresh air and felt even better. He turned his face up to the sun, feeling woozy. How long had he been in captivity? Days or weeks? He had no idea.

"Come on," Fortunata said.

He walked beside her, surprised but pleased to see a lot of the locals waiting outside to join the small search party heading toward the port. He recognized many people from the courtroom. They waved, and he waved back to them.

146

At the docks, Ebba was waiting for him with a bowl of porridge. He slurped it up as he walked. She looked ecstatic and said, "I've got all my female parts now, thanks to this case. I'm a woman!"

"Congratulations," he said.

"Court sessions have been suspended pending our return," Ebba said, which probably explained why Denny was being treated as though he were some famous explorer and not a pirate. Women handed him puddings and cakes, winking at him.

"There's more where that came from when you bring back our prince," they said.

"Wait," Denny said, handing the porridge bowl back to Ebba so he could hold onto his gifts. "Did you say pending our return?"

"Oh, yes. Barthelmass and I are coming with you. He's your ship's master."

"Good. I trust him."

She nodded. "We assembled your crew. They're all good men." She lowered her voice. "And none of them are under Fortunata's sway."

They boarded a sloop that had seen better days. Denny met his crew and was a little surprised that Fortunata was coming with him, but then, she was eager to see her brother and probably wasn't willing to let Denny out of her sight.

"You forgot to acknowledge one of the crewmembers," Ebba admonished him.

"I did?" He turned and saw a cat standing beside Fortunata, whose cheeks flamed.

"Theodore!" Denny dumped all the puddings and cakes onto the deck and picked up the cat. For once, Theodore didn't resist being cuddled. He stuck his head under Denny's chin and purred. "Where have you been?" Denny implored.

"I took him," Fortunata said.

Denny wanted to make her walk the plank.

"Stop that." She wagged a finger at him. "Don't forget I

147

can read your thoughts."

"You stole my cat!"

"I thought he was a sorcerer's cat, but he's a bit of a buffoon." She grinned. "Just like you."

"But I love him. I was really upset when I found out he'd disappeared."

"My brother loves him too. Theodore's gone half mad without him. Don't look at me like that. I didn't put your cat in chains!"

Denny rolled his eyes and put the cat back down on the deck. Theodore sniffed at the puddings, which clearly contained no fish, and walked away in disgust. He found a patch of sun and flopped onto the deck, flexing his claws.

"Okay," Denny said. "Let's plot our travel."

"Do you know where Rigby would take my brother?"

"I think so," he said. He didn't know why but from the moment she'd told him Rigby had abducted Merritt, the idea had come to him. Now, he was certain he was right.

"They're in Cornwall," he said. "I'm certain of it."

Fortunata looked astonished. "Cornwall? Why would they go there?" She furrowed her brow. "Why would *anybody* go there?"

"It's beautiful," Denny responded.

"No it's not."

"Yes it is!"

"Whereabouts in Cornwall?"

Denny hesitated. "Penzance."

"Oh my God. That place is horrible!"

"No. It is not."

"Yes it is!" She jabbed a finger at him. "Do you know what Penzance means?" Before he could respond she said, "It means wrecking. Charming, don't you think?"

"I love it. And wrecking is what pirates do. There's a lot of us who have bought homes there. One day they'll write songs about us. You wait and see."

"In your dreams."

"Do you want me to find your brother or not?"

148

"Yes, I do. And if you keep arguing with me, there's still time for me to condemn you to a lifetime of slavery."

Denny said nothing. He turned to Barthelmass, his new first mate. "I need maps of the North Atlantic sea ports for the United Kingdom. Please bring me anything you can find." Denny stared out at the ocean.

"Why do you think Rigby is in Penzance?" Fortunata asked as they waited. Her tone had turned gentle, so he responded in kind.

"A few of us bought houses there." Denny couldn't help the bitterness creeping into his tone. "Rigby and I were friends then. Our ship's doctor, Fellows, also bought a place there. I realize now that even he conspired against me." He stopped speaking, brooding over his circumstances.

"Try flying around," Fortunata said.

"Excuse me?"

"Try flying. You can't get far but it will make you feel better."

Ebba appeared and nodded at him in an encouraging way.

"But I don't know how."

"Flap your wings and imagine flying upward," Fortunata said.

Denny hesitated. "Is this a trick?"

"Boy, you don't think much of me, do you?"

Now he was afraid. She was really angry and he imagined her smiting him with her invisible brand of mean magic. "I don't think much of most people," he responded. "I can't help it. I'm a buffoon."

She laughed, and so did Ebba. Fortunata snapped her fingers and another woman hurried up the ladder from below deck. She was young and blonde and reminded Denny of his sister with her hesitant air and the nervous way she stood on the deck with them. She would have been attractive were it not for the huge warts all over her face. There were so many, some of the warts had their own warts growing from them.

149

"Is this your handiwork?" Denny asked Fortunata.

Fortunata looked at him. "What? The wings?"

"No. Those hideous warts."

"She was born with those," Fortunata muttered under her breath.

Ooops.

"This is Anisse." Fortunata rose again as she gestured to the blonde, whose cheeks had turned bright pink. "She's my lady-in-waiting. I gave her wings when she sewed the hem of my skirt too short."

"Sorry, m'lady." Anisse's cheeks turned so red Denny wondered why they hadn't caught fire.

Denny felt really bad now and hadn't recovered from his gaffe about the warts. He made some throwaway comment about, "Wings are wonderful, and yours are so pretty, Anisse."

"Try yours out, Denny," Fortunata said. "You can only go a few hundred feet in the air, but you'll see it's a gift that well serves you when we're out on the water."

If you say so. He looked up at the sky. *How am I supposed to fly?* Every time he tried to imagine it he wanted to laugh. He'd managed it a little in the prison cell, rising off his feet a few inches, but out here, it was hopeless.

"Anisse is going to help you. That's why I sent for her." Fortunata gestured to her lady-in-waiting. "Go on. Help the pirate fairy."

Denny couldn't help feeling that she was enjoying his ineptitude, and was about to say something when Anisse grabbed his hand.

"Fly with me, Denny!" she trilled and dragged him up into the air.

He'd always been afraid of heights. Come to think of it, he was afraid of water too and couldn't swim. Not that he'd ever let on to his crew. His mouth fell open in a long and silent scream but suddenly his wings were beating and his heart stopped trying to smash its way out of his chest, and he was flying!

"Oh!" He looked down, surprised at how serene and fragrant it was up here. He'd never smelled clouds before, or seen such dazzling colors beneath his feet. *I should have been born a bird.*

"Keep flapping your wings," Anisse instructed. "Think of it as treading waters, except you're doing it in the air."

He did as she'd suggested and it worked. His body felt weightless and filled with joy. He turned somersaults, making himself laugh. Anisse gripped his hand as he twirled upside down and around and around, but she did not move with him.

"Such a show-off," she shouted, but she didn't look angry. She flew with him up to the crow's nest, the upper part of the ship's main mast.

He and his crew often took turns sitting in the nest, but he frequently appointed others due to extreme fear. That didn't seem to be an issue now and he fell in love with the ability to fly up here like this on the spot. He knew he'd be coming up here often to get away from Fortunata, then realized she could probably fly, too. The sudden memory of her as a wizened old witch came to mind and he banished the thought. It was too beautiful a day to think such creepy things.

"So," Anisse said, as they perched in the crow's nest, which was the bottom portion of an old barrel. "Tell me quickly. Did she really give me warts?"

Denny looked at her, taken aback. "You mean you weren't born with those?"

Anisse's eyes glistened with tears. "Of course not. She lied. She always lies."

"And you didn't know you had warts?"

"She hasn't let me look in a mirror for three years. When I touch my face, I feel nothing." She gazed at him, her expression anxious. "Are they really bad?"

"Dreadful."

"Yours aren't exactly becoming either," she said with a sniff.

Denny gaped. "I have warts?" He reached up to feel them.

"Don't touch. She can't hear us up here. You've only got three, but they do attract attention."

"That conniving—"

Anisse put a hand on his arm. "She does it to everyone who's hexed and under an obligation to her."

"And you had no clue about your warts?" a dumbfounded Denny asked.

"No. And nobody else mentioned it. You're the first. The warts pile on after several days. She removes them when you complete a required task."

Denny looked at her. "And what's your required task?"

"I'm the go-between with her and the man she loves."

"Who is the man she loves?"

"Fellows. Your ship's doctor."

"Fellows? And she calls *me* a buffoon."

"We have to get down," Anisse whispered as Fortunata called up to them.

"What's taking so long?" She waved her arms, looking like a deranged albatross.

"You're going to have to pretend to try flying farther away," Anisse warned. "You won't succeed. You'll fall."

"And why would I do that?"

"It would be your natural instincts. I suppose you believed her when she said that Rigby kidnapped Merritt."

"Ahoy there!"

"What do you mean? Are you saying he wasn't kidnapped?"

"Of course not. Haven't you noticed her magic still works? I'll admit she has limited scope without him, but she got into a world of trouble sending him off to your ship, The Pirate Fairy. She'd read your thoughts, you know." Anisse dropped her gaze down to the deck where Fortunata was having a right royal hissy fit.

"Why did she do that?" Denny was feeling very stupid now and he didn't like the feeling at all.

"She read your thoughts and knew that you had gold

hidden in crevices all over the ship. She wanted it."

"What's going on up there?" Fortunata roared.

"It's Carpathian gold, isn't it?" Anisse whispered.

"Some of it. Yeah. Why?"

"You don't know?"

"Know what?"

"Boy. You *are* a buffoon."

"Shut up! I am not."

"Are too. Carpathian gold is bewitched." Her voice dropped farther until it was almost impossible to hear her. "It multiplies."

Denny gaped at her. *Boy, I am a buffoon.* "It does?"

She rolled her eyes. "The longer you have it, the more it self-duplicates. Fortunata has blown through her entire inheritance. She's been searching for Carpathian gold for years. She couldn't find any of your gold. She invaded one ship, not expecting to be abducted by the pirated Charlotte. When she got onto your ship, she looked everywhere for your gold. She knew it was there from reading your thoughts but couldn't locate it."

"Of course not." The notion infuriated him. "I've got that loot well hidden."

"Anyway, she sent poor Merritt to find it and Captain Rigby is holding him hostage."

"He's not a captain. He's a first mate!"

"Fortunata's powers dwindle when she and her brother are separated, and if one of them is in chains."

My God. I have those coins stuffed in caves and in my house in Penzance. Penzance! I'm taking Fortunata there! She'll steal all my money. The thought didn't bother him as much as the idea of something happening to Merritt. Denny would never forget what the man had already been through, and Denny cared more about Merritt than money. *What if Rigby hurts him? I don't trust him at all.*

"Get down here now!" Fortunata screamed.

Denny remembered how pitiful she had been when he

and his crew had first encountered her and Merritt on the Charlotte. *Of course!* Once Merritt had been unchained and started to recover, she'd seemed to materialize clothes and food out of nowhere.

"Now fly!" Anisse shoved him none too gently out of the crow's nest. "What are you doing?" she called aloud. "You can't go farther!"

Poor Denny started to plummet fast, unused to flying. Fearing a painful thud on the deck, he flapped his wings and headed for the skies again as Fortunata yelled his name.

"Denny!"

He hit his head on something. An invisible ceiling. Boy, did it hurt. It made him dizzy and winded him. He dropped down to the deck, all three women screaming as he landed like a dead bird.

Denny heard voices but couldn't raise himself physically, or ward off the strange, yet alluring dream in which he found himself. Denny was in a place where there was no pain.

"You gave him too much!" a female voice said from somewhere in the distance.

"It was never a problem before," another disembodied voice responded.

Denny turned around on the floor, but he was no longer outside. He was inside and to his astonishment he was in Christoph's private office at the jail in Tarragona. He couldn't recall a time, ever, where Christoph had lounged, naked on his brown leather sofa and beckoned Denny toward him, but that was what Christoph did now. His thick, huge, hard cock lay against his thigh and Christoph smiled.

"I won't bite. Ah, I see. You're in love with him. Do you know how long she's been keeping you captive?"

Christoph spoke better English than Denny remembered. "How long?" he asked.

"She can answer better than I." Christoph sat up now, looking off to his right with a frightened expression on his face. "I'm not supposed to fraternize with people stuck between life and death,

154

but I wanted to urge you not to die. You need to live. For both of us."

"Are you dead?" A sudden stab of anguish tore at Denny's heart.

"Oh, yes. It's been a few years now. Your captain killed me. You were supposed to die in my custody but I loved you. I couldn't bring myself to do it."

Denny sat up on the floor. *"No wonder I couldn't find you whenever I went back to Tarragona."*

Christoph nodded. *"I have to go. I'm sorry for us. For you. You have to go back, but whatever you do, don't listen to her. You can never return to that island. Merritt's sister means to kill you both. She wants only money. I'm to blame. I followed your progress and knew you'd captured a fortune in Carpathian gold. She wanted it, and is prepared to go to any lengths to get it."*

"How do you know her?" Denny was stumped by all of this.

"She was the woman I married. She was the wife I told you about. Please don't grieve my passing. Death was a mercy." Christoph blew him a kiss, and a strong, blinding white swamped the vision in front of Denny's eyes. Footsteps clattered from somewhere...

"Denny! Denny!" a woman's voice cried, luring Denny out of his dream.

"Polly?" he called out.

"Don't say my name! Save me!"

"Poll—" Her name died on his lips. Where is she? Who has her?

He knew then. He knew everything. Merritt's face swam into his mind. They were together. The man he loved and the sister he adored. Denny knew that Fortunata had sent Merritt to rescue Polly. *He would never have left me for gold. She must have made some bargain with him.* He could almost hear her saying, *Bring the sister, bring the gold, and I will let him live. I will let you be happy.*

"You know me so well," a voice whispered in his mind.

Denny gasped but dared not say Merritt's name.

Merritt was now lying naked on the couch in the same position Christoph had been. He arched an eyebrow toward Denny.

155

"Aren't you happy to see me?"

Denny swallowed. "Are you real?"

"If you believe I am, then I'm real."

An exhausted Denny looked at him. "I don't know what's real anymore. All I have is you and Polly, and I am nowhere near you."

"We're alive and we're waiting for you. Don't drink anymore nectar. My sister's been poisoning you." Merritt stopped speaking and cocked an ear to the left, a startled look on his face. "They promised me more time."

"Are you okay? Has Rigby hurt you?"

There was a sigh from Merritt. "I'm waiting for you."

Denny knew Merritt was waiting for him. Somewhere. Out there. In the world. "And I wait for you. I love you."

"Then you do believe." Merritt's face darkened. "It's been so long."

"Can I touch you?" Denny begged.

"Yes. But it's not enough time." He kept staring at the growing light coming for them.

"It will never be enough time." Denny crawled over to him, his sights set on the gorgeous mouth smiling at him and the luscious cock resting against Merritt's thigh.

The footsteps grew closer and Denny's body lifted before he could get any closer to Merritt.

"I love you!" Merritt shouted as Denny became blinded by the harsh white light.

He found himself on the deck again.

Merritt. Had it all been a trick? He opened his eyes, not wanting to see anything else but the man he loved.

"How long have I been held captive?" Denny asked as Ebba, Fortunata and Anisse hovered over him, exchanging glances. None of them responded. "Tell me," he croaked.

"Two years, seven months," Ebba said.

Denny was glad he was already lying down, otherwise he would have fallen over.

"You almost died," Fortunata whispered. "That wasn't supposed to happen." She looked worried and began pacing the deck, leaving Ebba and Anisse to raise him to his feet.

"I'll get you some nectar," Ebba said.

"No. No nectar."

Ebba shot an apprehensive glance toward Fortunata.

"Don't look at her. Listen to me. I can't get us to England if I'm out of my mind on drugs."

Fortunata's head snapped in his direction, her eyes dangerous slits. She stomped back over to him. "Who did you talk to on the other side?"

"Nobody," he lied.

"What did you see? There is no way you could have known your nectar had been bewitched unless someone told you."

Denny brushed off his clothes and gave her a tight smile. "I guessed," he said, wagging a finger at her. "You're good. I'll give you that. You had me fooled. I really thought I was in that cell for just a few days. And you'd better remove my warts and the ones on Ebba's and Anisse's faces too or — "

Ebba uttered a shriek, her hands flying to her face.

Denny went on with all the dignity he could muster. "If you don't stop with the stupid hexes and the poisoning, I will never, *ever* let you touch my gold."

Fortunata stared at him. "Who told you?"

Denny just threw back his head and laughed.

Chapter Eleven

Denny charted his course with his crew members. Barthelmass, Ebba, the quartermaster, bosun, rigger, ship's doctor, three sailors, Theodore the cat and even the customary cabin boy, a young stowaway who'd somehow escaped the island, were all informed of the ship's journey. Denny had always allowed his crew to be a part of the decision-making process. Denny had always prided himself on being strong enough to lead his team that was unruly but not so bloodthirsty that they killed him or abandoned him...or sold him off to what they thought were pirate ships.

As the ship set sail for Algeciras, in Spain, its first port of call, the mood on board was jubilant. Fortunata had been allowed to listen to the plans without offering an opinion.

"I don't trust you," Denny told her repeatedly. "And don't try bewitching anybody on board, or I'll make you walk the plank."

"Watch how you talk to me," she said, which really made him laugh. The stronger he acted, the more her powers seemed to recede.

Two years, seven months, he kept reminding himself. Had she not been running out of money she would have kept him imprisoned forever.

She sulked on her own, reduced to the task of swabbing the deck, per Denny's instructions. The crew took turns monitoring her.

"And use no poison, mind," Barthelmass admonished her.

Ebba went below deck to make Denny more porridge. She

promised it wouldn't be poisoned, and Denny was forced to believe her.

They had a three-week journey ahead of them, and the crew remained in good spirits, especially when it seemed that the food on board was pretty good.

"She can't make food appear by magic," Ebba informed Denny. "Somehow she's lost all her powers. She is afraid of you."

"Good."

"Who did you see when you hovered between life and death?"

Merritt's face loomed in his mind. "An angel. That's all you need to know."

Ebba nodded and handed him a huge bowl of porridge. Denny felt sure Fortunata had sent her to ask him this question, but Denny had no need to divulge his secrets. He kept his mind blank and focused on the task at hand, getting to Cornwall.

For several days, the voyage went smoothly until they weathered a bad storm on the eleventh day. Fortunata, Ebba, Barthelmass and Bertie, the cabin boy, all took to their beds, slumbering like dormice, avoiding the ship's wild surges. Denny loved it, as did the rest of his crew. He was surprised that Anisse handled it so well, but though she tried, her cooking was grim. She couldn't help burning everything that came into her path. She was, however, an excellent seamstress and did a bang-up job patching torn sails and clothing.

In the middle of one particularly violent sea squall, Christoph came to him in his mind.

"Guard your thoughts," Christoph warned. *"Trust nobody."* He then went on to give Denny surprising instructions. He yearned to talk to somebody about the surprising visit from Christoph, but knew he couldn't. He was just anxious to hit dry land to execute the first of his plans. Plans he had to keep shielded from Fortunata.

* * * *

The longer Denny was at sea, and the more time he had to think about the past, the more some things started to make sense. One day, while out on deck looking across the ocean with a spyglass, Ebba came to him. She seemed happy now that she'd recovered from motion sickness and was back in the kitchen, cooking.

"Is everything all right?" she asked him.

Denny watched a whale breaching in the distance, the joyful moment spoiled when distaste flooded his mouth at the sound of her words.

"Yes, and you can tell the witch if she has a question to come and ask me herself."

Ebba looked at him. "But she's a princess. You must be nicer to her."

"Really?" He shook his head. "Has it worked for you?"

"Of course." She looked wary then. "Why? What's going on?"

"She's put the warts back on your nose."

Ebba's hands flew to her face and her mouth fell open in a strangled cry. They were all over her cheeks and nose. "Fortunata!" she screamed, running for the ladder.

Good. That'll put the cat among the pigeons. Denny wasn't afraid of Fortunata's wrath. He was sick of her. If Christoph's messages were correct, then change was afoot. Change that everybody except Fortunata would like.

He raised the spyglass back to his eye, but the whale was gone.

In the distance, he spotted two boats. Fishing boats, likely. He flew up to the crow's nest and kept an eye on them. An hour later, young Bertie joined him, climbing with ease up the flagpole.

"There are two Spanish fishing boats out there," the child informed him. "Can I fire the cannons, sir?"

"No, you cannot."

"Aw. What kind of pirate are you anyway?" Bertie asked,

his hopeful glance falling into dismay.

"The regular kind. Who suggested firing the cannons, anyway?"

"Fortunata. She promised me lollies if I blew up those boats."

"Go to the kitchen and ask Ebba to boil you some lollies. Tell her I said to do it and that it's a most urgent matter."

Bertie's face brightened. "Really? I can do that?"

"You have my permission. Do you like treacle toffee?"

Bertie looked moon-faced. "I've never tried it."

"She makes the best treacle toffee in the world. Mention that to her when you ask her nicely to make her some."

"You're the best dread pirate I've ever met!" Bertie hurled his arms around Denny, who laughed.

"I'm the only pirate you've met, aren't I?"

"A bit."

"A bit?"

"I met Pirate Captain Rigby."

"He's not a captain. He's a second mate!"

"Huh. He says he's a captain. He took my father on his ship and left me on the island. 'Tis a stinky island, isn't it?"

Denny nodded. "I thought so. Now climb down and get yourself some toffee."

"Aye, aye, Captain! Sir!" Bertie managed a salute as he shimmied back down the pole. Suddenly the two fishing boats in the distance vanished. Now that was strange.

Denny didn't have much time to worry about it. Barthelmass appeared on the deck.

"We have a fire in the boiler room," he shouted up to Denny.

"No, we don't. Go down to Fortunata and tell her to quit clowning around. Tell her no more fires, no more fishing boats, or I'll make her scrub every inch of this tub!"

Barthelmass looked at him, bug-eyed. "You really want me to say all that to her?"

"Yes, I really want you to say all that to her," Denny mimicked. "*Now.*"

His dark tone sent Barthelmass scurrying below deck. Denny was in a bad mood now. He flew back down to the deck, pacing. He emptied his mind of all thoughts. It was no good letting her rub him up the wrong way and delve into his mind. He knew just the thing to stop her antics and went below deck. The pleasing smell of treacle streamed from the galley. Little Bertie was laughing, and when Denny poked his head into the galley, he saw that the lad was eating a piece of fried bread as he sat atop the table.

The boy's cheeks flamed and he scuttled down to the floor. "Sorry, sir."

"Don't apologize." Denny was exhausted. The truth was, all the secrecy and thought-guarding was taking its toll on Denny.

He sat on the long bench at the table, Bertie moving beside him. The child seemed cold. Denny didn't say anything. Maybe it was because he forced himself to sleep in increments at night, circling the ship at odd hours to keep an eye on Fortunata. He started to doze when he received an unexpected visit in his mind. This time it was the twin seers from the jury.

They spoke in unison, but with perfect clarity. He held his breath as they gave him instructions. They suddenly vanished. When he blinked and opened his eyes again, Fortunata was standing in front of him, hands on hips.

"Sleeping on the job, Captain?" she sneered.

He looked up at her. "Something like that." He smiled at her, knowing his secrecy rattled her. Her uncertain gaze shifted from side to side.

"And you, cabin boy. Go make my bed." She pointed to Bertie, who stopped eating.

Denny watched him a moment. The kid was frightened but there was something about the child...a defiance Denny admired.

Fortunata in turn stared at Denny, who blocked his thoughts from her.

"Be kind, Fortunata. He's a mere boy."

162

She flared her nostrils but stopped short of a response. Every chance she got, Fortunata bossed Bertie around, especially when she thought Denny wasn't near them. Ebba pulled Denny aside to report Fortunata's behavior, but he shrugged it off.

"This isn't like you." Ebba seemed stunned. "You are the one who always protects women and children."

"I know," he said. "Say, do we have any toffee left?" Denny didn't want to hear about any shipboard dramas.

Over the coming days, he took to giving Bertie errands away from Fortunata and making sure they were never left alone together. In their final week before they arrived at Algeciras, Denny stepped up his nighttime patrols of the ship. Twice he caught Fortunata attempting to enter Bertie's cabin and so he moved the boy into a cabin with the rigger and gunner, instructing them to shoot Fortunata if she tried entering their quarters.

Denny was so tense by the time they arrived at the port, he could hardly see straight. When they docked, he asked Fortunata to accompany him ashore. He made sure visions of coins, lots and lots of lovely Carpathian coins danced in his head. She saw them of course and her eyes gleamed with predatory joy. Denny instantly guarded his thoughts again and mentally rubbed his hands. He invited Bertie and Anisse ashore with them. As the crew members drifted off in different directions, Denny's small party accompanied him through the main plaza a few feet away from the ocean.

Denny thought Algeciras was one of the ugliest ports he'd visited over the years, but he could have hugged the place, so grateful was he to be on dry land. Bertie ran over to Los Arcos, the public fountain, and ran his hands through the water.

"Fresh water," the boy kept saying and suddenly jumped into it.

Denny and the others hauled him out, but Bertie was good natured about his brief romp.

The square had been improved since Denny had last

been here, marked off with chains attached to stone posts. Poplars and a plethora of palm trees bordered the square. The sudden burst of orange blossom tickled Denny's nose. Young Bertie snagged an orange from one of the many trees planted in wooden boxes in the square and held it to his face.

"Oh. A fresh orange," he murmured over and over again.

Denny almost felt sorry for him. He led his group toward the entrance to the *Rastro de Sabado*—Saturday Market—where they found busty, colorfully dressed women selling everything from embroidered shirts and dresses to thick slices of *pan de la casa*—house bread—topped with tomato, ham, and baked and drizzled with olive oil. Denny treated them to some as they toured the tables where Moroccan sailors sold antique furniture and trinkets that looked they'd been stolen. There were also some questionable fellows selling dirty clothes and rusty tools.

People stared at Denny, pointing at his wings, but he ignored them.

"This place is amazing," Anisse said, her face alight at the rich colors of yarns and fabrics on display.

He encouraged her to buy, slipping coins into her hand. When he was certain the others weren't looking, he walked away, past the old man selling ugly stones with odd images painted on them with gouache. Everything he painted, whether it was a tree or a house, had a human face somewhere in it. And the human face had demonic eyes. The old man made money because his work was weird, but Denny slipped him some gold, declining to take one of the stones.

The old man's fingers closed around Denny's as he took the coins. "You're back," he said.

Denny resisted the urge to say, "No, I am not." He smiled at the old man who had no sense of humor but kept an eye on Denny's treasure. He moved along a cobbled street and, checking over his shoulder to ensure he wasn't being followed, Denny turned into a tiny alleyway. For a moment, he stopped. Time had stood still since his last visit. The little corner was still filled with tall, whitewashed buildings that had seen better days. They'd each been separated into little apartments with their windows open and the inhabitants milling about inside. Denny paused to inhale the smell of oranges, freshly washed clothes hanging on lines strung between the buildings, coffee and something else. *Hope.* He glanced around. Somebody was playing Spanish guitar. *Guitarra Latina* they called it. The guitar of the common people.

He darted into the narrow passageway between two of the buildings and tried to focus on his quest. *She's here.* He felt her presence, took a deep breath and plunged down another narrow pathway. He stopped at the place with the red door. Many places painted their doors red to ward off evil. Too bad it hadn't worked this time. He opened the door, walked inside and ran straight through the house. In the back room, he opened another door and stepped into a tiny storage room and waited a fraction of a second before pushing open a space that looked like a thin line between two bricks. It worked. He went inside and found the same claustrophobic, dank room he'd encountered before. The priest hole. He felt along the bricks and was stunned that his gold was still there. And, boy, it had really multiplied.

And to think I contemplated banking it with goldsmiths! He stuffed his leather pouch and three satin ones Anisse had sewn for him near the start of their voyage. Weighed down with gold, he turned to find Fortunata right behind him.

"What are you doing here?" He feigned surprise, but wasn't sure if she believed him. The room was still dark and he made his way out, even as she grabbed him.

"You can't hide from me!" she screamed.

"I'm not trying to hide."

"You can't run, either."

He left the room, shutting the door. Fortunata shouted in frustration, beating her fists against it. She couldn't make it open. He ran then, but Fortunata was soon close on his heels, Bertie behind him. Where had he come from? Had he released her? In the alleyway, Anisse stood with a bolt of purple silk over her shoulder.

"Get back to the ship," he yelled. "I'll explain."

She didn't skip a beat. She turned and moved as fast as she could under the weight of the fabric. Denny ran straight ahead, Fortunata literally breathing down his neck. Her claw-like talons emerged and grabbed him. He knew he had to get her to the good witch before Fortunata destroyed him.

He barreled into the door he'd seen in the dream sent by the twin seers from Fortunata's island. The door had been marked with a pentagram in oil. He jumped through the entrance, Fortunata and Bertie right behind him.

Two men grabbed Fortunata, who shrieked and writhed. A ghostly figure emerged from the dark recesses of the room.

"Gremma!" Fortunata spat out the word. "What are *you* doing here?"

Denny couldn't help staring. This Gremma person was the spitting image of the twin seers. She must have been the third sister. Triplets. She looked exactly like them save for a couple of hideous warts on her face.

"I can't believe she's here." Gremma kept staring at Fortunata. "Change me back, and all this will go away."

One of the men released her right arm, and Fortunata pointed a withered finger at her. The warts vanished.

"Arrest her." Gremma told the man who grabbed her again. "She cast spells on me, her own brother and everyone else in our kingdom."

"You said you'd make it go away," Fortunata hollered.

"And I am, though probably not the way you expected." She turned to Denny. "What do you want me to do with her?"

"Keep her here. Under heavy guard. I bring you Carpathian gold."

166

Gremma seemed surprised. "I've never seen this before. And it really multiplies?"

Denny nodded. "Oh, yes."

Gremma sat down, as though exhausted. "You just want me to hold her?"

"No. I want you to remove her deadly powers. Put a spell on her that makes her do only good. And if she tries to do something wicked, she gets a boil on her bottom and a wart on her face."

"No!" Fortunata squealed.

"I like that idea." Gremma played with the coins now, mesmerized. "And maybe the boils cannot be removed. If she wants them removed, she loses a year of her life."

"You're not as nice as your sisters," Denny observed.

"She cursed me twenty-three years ago and banished me from the palace. I'm a little...annoyed."

Denny nodded. "I can understand that. We will stay in touch. Once you inform me that she is fully cured, Prince Merritt and I will come for her."

Gremma gave him a lovely smile. "That may take a very long time."

"Fine by me. Oh. There's one more thing. Please make her remove the hex on this child, Bertie."

"I'm hexed?" Bertie looked befuddled.

"But who is he?" Gremma asked.

"I'm not sure, but I detected the chill of bewitchment around him. And I suspect he's Arthur Fellows, my former ship's doctor. He's in love with her." Denny gestured to Fortunata, then down to Bertie. "He's an idiot." He glanced down at Bertie. "No offense, Bertie."

The boy shrugged.

"And what about you?" Gremma asked. "Can I remove your wings?"

"You can do that?" Denny hadn't counted on that bit of good news.

"Oh, yes. I'm the most powerful witch in the universe. That's why she did this to me. She tricked me and I fell for

167

it."

"You can remove my wings." Denny had never been so relieved in his life. It was almost climactic when the seer waved her hand and the wings vanished from his body. He breathed a bit easier and smiled at Fortunata.

"I'll get you for this," Fortunata snarled at Denny.

"Can you remove the wings from her lady-in-waiting, Anisse?" Denny asked.

"I can." Gremma nodded. "I just need something she has touched." Her hand fell on one of the silk purses. "She made this?"

"Yes." *Boy, she is good.*

"Consider it done." The seer reached over and shook his hand. "I will need to keep Fortunata imprisoned to counteract all the wrongs she has done. It will take at least a year, unless you were thinking of my keeping her here longer?"

"Yes, two years and seven days," Denny said.

Gremma smiled. "The same amount of time she kept you imprisoned. By the time I'm through with her she'll be so sweet she will give you toothache."

"No, I won't." Fortunata glowered at her.

Gremma ignored her and gestured to the two men who dragged the weeping Fortunata away.

When she'd gone, Bertie fell asleep in a chair.

"He will awaken shortly and will remember none of what happened to him." Gremma said, "You've done a very kind thing." She paused. "How are my sisters?"

"They are wonderful. They miss you very much."

The seer looked overcome with emotion. "I will contact them and let them know I've regained my powers. I've been so limited, thanks to Fortunata."

"I wish you well," Denny said. "And now, I must return to my ship."

He took the last of the remaining coins from the priest hole and hastened back to port. His crew was rushing back with fresh provisions. Only Ebba seemed upset that Fortunata

168

had been arrested.

She sighed. "Fortunata made life so interesting."

"No, she made it scary," Denny retorted. He begged the crew to hurry with their repairs and the replenishment of their stocks.

The following day they left for the port of Plymouth, and Denny got used to life without wings again.

"What do you miss the most?" Anisse asked him over breakfast one morning.

"Being able to fly up to the crow's nest. My knees aren't what they used to be."

"Me too. But at least we have the memories. Most people don't even have those to look back upon on a chilly morning."

"Aye, 'tis true." Denny studied his maps. He felt whatever he had to face in Penzance was worth everything he had to go through to rescue Merritt. He'd chosen Plymouth as the port at which they'd dock, but hadn't counted on running into The Pirate Fairy at sea. Denny and his crew had first spotted her at daybreak and had laughed when they'd seen the ship had been attacked by a whale. She was sinking.

Denny and his crew offered everybody safe passage, but Captain Rigby refused to leave his ship.

"Fortunata can fix it," Rigby said. "Where is she?"

"Imprisoned."

Rigby looked shocked.

"Where is my sister?" Denny demanded.

"At his house, in Penzance," one of Rigby's crewmen responded.

"And Merritt?"

"He's there too."

"You traitor," Rigby said, and lunged at the sailor.

Denny swung his way onto Rigby's ship and fought him, first by sword, then pointed the gun Fortunata had given him. Half expecting it not to work, Denny fired, but Rigby jumped overboard, straight into the path of a circling school of sharks. Rigby didn't even have time to scream,

169

they devoured him on sight.

* * * *

Three days later, Denny and his crew arrived at Plymouth and loaded up with fresh supplies before heading to Cornwall. They rented horses and buggies to travel by road to Rigby's house. Merritt and Polly were nowhere to be seen, but Rigby's men came out and gave no resistance to Denny. It was a good thing too. He'd been a good boss to Sorenson and Foster. They seemed pleased to see him too. They accepted his gold coins and took off for some parade down on Market Jew Street.

"It's St. Piran's Day," Foster said.

"Never mind that, where's my sister?"

"She's in the kitchen, cooking." Foster looked embarrassed. "Prince Merritt's in the bedroom. He's sleeping. They both sleep a lot. Is Fortunata really in prison?"

"Yes, she is. And she's been turned into a good witch."

"I'll believe that when I see it," Foster said and hurried down to the parade.

Denny found Polly in the kitchen. She was darning a sock and looked up, surprise, then pleasure crossing her features when she saw Denny.

"Is it really you?" Her voice cracked, as though she couldn't believe her own eyes.

"You look beautiful," he said.

They ran to each other. He hugged her hard.

"Did I just die and go to heaven?" she asked.

"If you did, then so have I." He touched her face and hair. She was Polly. Still the same girl. Older, but still the sister he loved.

"How did you find me?" Tears pooled in her eyes.

"It's taken me years. Are you all right, Poll?"

"I am...now. Denny. I've missed you so much!" She burrowed her head under his chin.

"You're so tall," he murmured as they clung to each other.

"I'm not ten anymore," she said, though her voice sounded like that of a little girl.

He held her tighter. *I will never let her out of my sight again.* He held her, delighting in the sheer luxury of being with her again.

When they parted, they were both crying.

"There is so much to tell you," she said, swatting at her tears. "I don't know what kind of spell is upon us, but all I want to do is clean, cook and sleep."

"Take a rest for now and I'll find Prince Merritt, then we can all go to the parade."

"He's a very nice man. I really like him."

"I like him too." Denny never wanted to let her go, but she settled into a chair by the window, smiling as she slipped into sleep, her face in the sun. He would get her and Merritt away from here, away from whatever poison she'd been given. He hoped the seer's magic would soon work and the spell would be broken. He ran from room to room, searching for his lost love.

And there was Merritt, sleepy in bed, his eyes aglow when he saw Denny. "Am I dreaming?"

"No, darling, you are not."

When Merritt smiled, Denny didn't know what to say. His mind, body and soul melted into an insane puddle that made him say the daftest thing ever. "There's a parade. Please tell me we can leave this house and go join the fun."

"How did you know I love parades?" Merritt reached for him. "There's something we have to do first, though."

"There is?" Denny couldn't stop smiling.

"Oh, yes, there is." Merritt laughed as Denny threw himself across the bed and kissed him.

"No ropes for us today," Denny said. "I want both your hands on me."

"I want that too."

It felt so good to touch him again that Denny took his time just running his fingers across every inch of skin.

Merritt seemed to come back to life, got up and kicked

the door shut. "I know what's different. You've lost your wings."

Denny laughed. "Your sister can no longer hurt us."

Merritt looked amazed. "Really?"

"Really." Denny grabbed him and took him down to the floor, trying to get between his legs.

Merritt twisted and turned underneath him as if fighting Denny, even as his hands held Denny's head to his. Their cocks connected. Denny's was rock hard, Merritt's was not.

"It's the sleeping potion," Merritt said.

Denny ground himself against him and Merritt's breath quickened. Denny pulled Merritt's shirt up and over his head, a couple of buttons popping off against the floor. He took hold of Merritt's left hand, licking and kissing the palm as his fingers flexed in pleasure. Denny stole a glance at Merritt's face as he sucked his fingertips, one by one. There was a look of disbelief as well as furious lust. Denny bent forward to lick his face and neck.

Merritt moaned as Denny moved down to his torso. As he traced Merritt's ribs with his tongue, Denny held Merritt's hands up over his head, and heard his deep, contented sigh. Denny kept rubbing, dry humping Merritt's crotch with his knee, and at last, Denny felt him harden. He reached up with another kiss for Merritt's mouth, one hand going to his swollen cock. He couldn't help himself. He needed to touch that sweet, thick, piece of manhood. He had the juiciest one Denny had ever seen, his balls heavy in his hands. He ran Merritt's cock head against his face. Merritt squirmed for entry into Denny's mouth, but Denny had to make him wait.

Denny tightened his grip on Merritt's cock, running it down his throat and to his chest. The second the head touched Denny's nipple, they both groaned. Denny took Merritt's pants all the way down past his feet. Merritt's fingers made quick work of Denny's pants, and as he inched the fabric past Denny's ass, Denny knew in seconds he was going to be inside Merritt, his man panting for a

172

hard pounding, his legs wrapped around Denny's waist.

No, Denny wanted this to last.

He kept rubbing Merritt's cock over his arms and face, licking his way down Merritt's thighs. His legs opened up. His body implored Denny, *fuck me*. But Denny kept at it, licking him, teasing him, tasting him. *Oh, yeah.*

His cock was in Denny's mouth now, and Merritt's gorgeous ass came off the floor. He flailed around as Denny sucked him thirstily. Merritt's cock adored Denny, and he kept a hold on Merritt as he started to come.

As soon as he was finished, Merritt's body still tensing, his pulse racing, Denny put his mouth straight down onto his ass. Merritt's feet rested on Denny's shoulders.

Merritt reached for him as Denny used Merritt's juices to prepare him for Denny's cock. Merritt touched Denny's cock with his fingertips. "I want it, I want it, I want it."

Prince Merritt's wish was Denny's command. He plunged into him, loving how tight Merritt was, how good it felt to fuck him. Finally. Merritt grabbed Denny's face, their mouths glued to one another. When they finally broke apart to breathe, Merritt said, "I love you, Denny."

"Merritt, I love you, too." He sobbed when they came together. It was perfect. It was bliss. It was better than dreams.

And it was better than any bleedin' parade.

HE THOUGHT HE WAS MOVING FOR A JOB...

INSTEAD
HE GOT A
LIFE

THE
BOUNCER

A. J. LLEWELLYN

The Bouncer

Excerpt

Chapter One

The sign on the portable corridor coming off the JetBlue flight read, *Welcome to Austin, Live Music Capital of the World.*

It cheered me up after the long, long wait in airports stretching from New York to Long Beach in California, not to mention the turbulent three-hour flight here. I took it as a good sign. I believed in signs. I've always looked for them and found them, good or bad. This was good. I loved music, live music in particular, and I was about to throw myself right into the music scene working for my brother.

To me, it was like a personalized welcome mat after being shuttled around the country due to inclement weather. I felt lucky that I'd made it. Seventy-two passengers had agreed to fly all over the country and even to Mexico to finally land in Austin and we'd decided we knew each other well enough to exchange numbers and promises of cocktails.

For several horrible hours, we'd circled first one New York airport, then another, and after a detour to New Jersey, had been left on the tarmac in Newark. Waiting. We hadn't been able to get to an arrival gate due to overcrowding. In an incident that made all the TV headlines, the flight attendants had run out of food and had rationed us to two peanuts per person and half a cup of water each.

JetBlue had rallied, saving the day. One of their planes heading to Florida had turned around and rescued us. A group of seasoned flight attendants had boarded our craft like the sexiest cavalry you ever saw, stampeding down the aisle carrying food, drink and bringing abundant good cheer. Among them had been my brother's husband, former boxer and now-flight attendant, Tito Calderon.

He'd picked me out right away and came straight over to me.

"This is a funny old way to meet," he'd said. "You doing okay, Kevin?"

To tell you the truth, like everybody else, I'd started to panic quite a long time ago. Especially when I'd seen the news of our unfolding melodrama on the screen in front of me, which of course magnified our predicament.

"I'm fine, Tito." I'd tried to act macho. Tito was hot. Hotter than hot. He radiated the kind of sexual chemistry that ought to be forbidden in real life. It should be left on the screen for guys whose names end in Clooney or Damon. I wondered how my brother coped with the attention magnetism like Tito's must bring.

Satisfied I was okay, Tito had given me a couple of bottles of iced water, several snack bags and moved on to help a breast-feeding mother handle her squalling baby.

I'd glimpsed his wedding ring. It made me feel good, for my brother's sake that he wasn't the kind of guy who took off his ring when he was a traveling man. I'd caught Tito's gaze and we'd smiled at each other. He'd taken charge of the screaming baby, handing a bottle to one of our frazzled, original flight attendants.

175

"Can you warm this for me, please? Thirty seconds ought to do it."

She'd looked as if she wanted to squeeze the contents all over his face. Instead, she snatched it and thundered her way back to the galley.

I had been able to hear her surly words. "Excuse me. Excuse me, please."

The new JetBlue crew had made instant TV headlines as they'd escorted us from the plane to one of their waiting buses across the snow-dusted tarmac. Tito had acted like he was used to having cameras on him and I'd wondered just how bad I looked.

Once he'd been sure I was safely on the bus headed back to New York, he'd given me a quick hug. I'd detected very faint aftershave. *Holy frickin' heck.* My dick had got hard. Was that bad when it was your brother's husband?

"See you back in Austin," he'd said. "I'll be home tonight."

I didn't think there was a happy person on that bus once we'd survived the bumpy two-hour bus ride—the driver had got lost—and arrived at La Guardia, just as our original plane was landing.

Another long wait. I wondered if I'd grown chest hair in the interim. The constant flight changes had even worn out the flight attendants who'd left a basket of cookies and snacks up front saying we should help ourselves. I'd tried to focus on reading something on my new Kindle, a gift from my mom. Instead, I'd become obsessed with the choppy digital TV service on my personal screen on the back of the seat in front of me. I'd watched an alarming array of reality programming. Some loopy, scary-looking plastic surgery nightmare of a housewife in Orange County, wherever the hell that was, went off on her husband because they couldn't afford their mortgage.

More books from
A.J. Llewellyn

World War Two brought them together…but a family's threat to take away Tinder and Jason's son, Christopher, could tear them apart.

TOTALLY BOUND

BEYOND
THE
Reef

Tony finds that
true love means
taking a leap
of faith.

A.J. LLEWELLYN

*Tony takes a shower one day and finds a naked man
fondling his loofah. Frank's a sex machine who knows
Tony's deepest desires…and won't go away.*

When Dr Jack Hanrahan set out for a much needed vacation, he had no idea his life would forever change on a remote biking trail in Roley's Wood…

He gets a wild encounter...in more ways than one...

The Kaupe

A.J. Llewellyn

Dino Perez is a super-hot Hollywood makeup artist who is used to dating the most gorgeous men in town.

About the Author

A.J. Llewellyn

A.J. Llewellyn lives in California, but dreams of living in Hawaii. Frequent trips to all the islands, bags of Kona coffee in the fridge and a healthy collection of Hawaiian records keep this writer refueled.

A.J. never lacks inspiration for male/male erotic romances and on the rare occasions this happens, pursues other passions such as collecting books on Hawaiiana, surfing and spending time with friends and animal companions.

A.J. Llewellyn believes that love is a song best sung out loud.

A.J. Llewellyn loves to hear from readers. You can find contact information, website details and an author profile page at https://www.pride-publishing.com/

PUBLISHING